F
Hunt, John
The blockhouse   19.99

THE BLOCKHOUSE

When Bob Carter stops at the settlement of Tumbleweed, he is arrested almost immediately by a not-so-honest sheriff. Effecting a dramatic escape, he has a chance encounter with a tame bear, and then its female owner. Even more surprises await the cowboy when, hired by the very woman who originally accused him of stealing her horse, Carter faces the prospect of a shotgun wedding — with a horse for reward. Enmeshed in this tangled web, Carter can see no way out. Only a bloody gunfight will clear the air!

JOHN HUNT

◆

THE BLOCKHOUSE

Complete and Unabridged

LINFORD
Leicester

First published in Great Britain in 2001 by
Robert Hale Limited
London

First Linford Edition
published 2002
by arrangement with
Robert Hale Limited
London

British Library CIP Data

Hunt, John, *1916 –*
    The blockhouse.—Large print ed.—
Linford western library
    1. Western stories
    2. Large type books
    I. Title
    813.5'4 [F]

    ISBN 0–7089–9882–8

Published by
F. A. Thorpe (Publishing)
Anstey, Leicestershire

Set by Words & Graphics Ltd.
Anstey, Leicestershire
Printed and bound in Great Britain by
T. J. International Ltd., Padstow, Cornwall

This book is printed on acid-free paper

1

Tumbleweed

The territory was hooded by great mountains, some overhanging, others sheared off straight up and down. Excepting for the sheer stone overhangs, the high country, even where it was not precipice, was forested. Pine trees part way up, fir trees at the higher places.

If a man rode southward, which was not easy in country so thickly wooded, there were waterways, some thunderous, full-flowing and marked by cascading places where the country was sufficiently broken to ensure riffles, some raucously noisy as they crashed over huge and ancient over-croppings.

Because water was important anywhere in the southwest there existed dangerous old trails where a misstep was deadly; the heights of those trails angled from a few feet above water to about a thousand feet of uninterrupted fall.

Mostly these ancient trails had been made by animals; moose, caribou, elk and deer, wolves, coyotes, bears and smaller creatures. The variety of wildlife included inedible critters, opossum, snowshoe rabbits, and lesser wildlife. Enough of it in this kind of territory to pretty well appear every few hundred yards. All a man needed was ammunition, a Winchester carbine and a gut withered from hunger and he could live a long time on the best kind of meat between Canada and Mexico.

In other ways it was a rich territory, but most folks moved around using wheeled vehicles, buggies, wagons or coaches, ways of getting around that required more or less flat country and roads.

If a rider sashayed in timbered country he might have a reason. That was why strangers coming south from the snow banks of Wyoming, Colorado and the northernmost parts of New Mexico used the trails between peaks; so he could get to know the high country before he abandoned it for flat land where folks settled, made ranches, villages and towns.

Ordinarily, a person in unfamiliar territory rode beside railroad tracks. Not always; if a rider preferred entering territory he wasn't familiar with and did not want to run across other folks.

The stocky-built horseman with pigeon wings of grey at the temples knew no one where he was travelling and for the time being would rather not encounter folks.

What he had seen from a bony ridge was a settlement and livestock country for as far as he could see, and a lot further.

He had over the years pictured in his mind the kind of place in which he would like to put roots down, and of all the places he had seen that had been visible from the knobby ridge, this might be it.

The town didn't grow near railroad tracks. From what he had seen from back yonder, the railroad tracks were about six or eight miles easterly. Possibly the folks in that settlement worked for the railroad, or maybe ran livestock. He had seen many grazing animals.

He came out of the upland timber country where a middling little creek flowed between bordering rows of creek-willows as thick as hair on a dog's back, facing the distant settlement.

He could have pushed his horse and arrived in that settlement ahead of sundown but he didn't. He had made camp in a hundred worse places than beside the creek. It would be supper-time in another couple of hours, so he selected a good spot, hobbled his pigeon-toed, muscled-up buckskin horse, settled his bedroll where he would sleep and being plumb certain there was no one around he stripped down and took a leisurely all-over-bath with only an irate and raucous flock of nesting birds upset by his presence.

He had a couple of hours to dry off in the privacy of his secluded place. He could not see out, and seeing in would require some effort. He had a towel, but he'd left it in the saddlebags. He didn't need it, the sun was losing its power but would not go behind the backgrounding mountains for another couple of hours.

He dragged his canvas ground-cloth to creek-side and stretched out. Because he meant to bed down in this place until morning he settled comfortably and napped.

The chill awakened him. It was dark, his horse had stocked up and was dozing out a short distance.

When he was awakened fully it was still dark but off in the east a wide sliver of fish-belly grey showed where dawn was taking its time about brightening a new day.

He was hungry. There were trout in

the creek but it would take awhile to catch and cook some of them and the town was closer; it would have an eatery.

The horse was ready and stepped out in the right direction as though he knew where his rider intended to go.

On the outskirts of the settlement, someone had placed a large rock to denote the town in bright red letters: Tumbleweed.

The horseman had been in his share of settlements. This one seemed to be cleaner than some of the others he'd been in.

He sought the livery barn, engaged the paunchy, elderly liveryman in conversation while his horse was being offered water at a stone trough, stalled and fed a generous feed box half full of rolled grain and a mangerful of hay.

The liveryman's name was Clyde Offen. He was a widower, had a daughter at school down at Santa Fe and it made Clyde rustle his stumps to send the money down there.

When Clyde pushed out his hand he said, 'Welcome to Tumbleweed, mister . . . used to be Indians and soldiers. They're all gone now.'

The stranger said his name as he pumped the liveryman's hand. 'Carter . . . Bob Carter.'

'Mister Carter,' Clyde said, as he pulled out his pocket watch and studied the spindly little black hands. When he finished the handshake, Clyde also said, 'We could visit, Mr Carter, except I haven't had m'breakfast yet.'

'Me neither, Mr Offen.'

Clyde smiled. 'Come along, Mr Carter. It's not like back East somewhere but it's fillin'.'

Carter returned the smile. 'It's just plain Bob, if you don't mind, Clyde.'

The eatery was plain with muslin curtains to block afternoon sun and a handsome widow-woman as the owner-operator. Her name was Kate Corrigan. She was attractive, with a head of dark auburn hair, dead level eyes and a wide rare smile. She had smiled until her husband Mike was killed when his stage went over a cliff at the place subsequently known as Corrigan's Bluff.

She welcomed old Clyde and the stalwart stranger with a welcome for the liveryman and a steady look at his youngish companion.

Clyde introduced them. Carter smiled, Kate Corrigan neither smiled nor spoke. Her gaze was steady as it settled on Clyde when she said, 'The usual, Clyde? Sourdough flapjacks?'

As she looked at the stranger he smiled and nodded. 'Sounds good.'

As they settled at the immaculate counter, Clyde bobbed his head and spoke. 'Black java, Katie.'

She went to the kitchen and called over her shoulder. 'The third time this month, Clyde. Pete took out of here an hour ago.'

'Third time, Kate?'

'Not only that but the doctor was told by Leary it was the same two.'

Clyde stiffened slightly where he sat. 'Katie . . . that's hard to believe.'

She evidently did not hear him. The massive old iron fry pan rattled boisterously so there was no answer. The liveryman turned to face Bob Carter and when he spoke his next comment was just barely audible. 'That's where her husband went over the edge a couple of years past.'

That ended the conversation. After the meal arrived there was no additional speech.

The liveryman noticed that Bob Carter stole several gazes at the widow-woman. Bob Carter smiled and followed the liveryman out into a dazzling morning which was close to being half spent. Back at the livery barn they rolled smokes, got comfortable and the liveryman only had two interruptions as the day wore along toward noon.

When the stranger finally went to the rooming-house in the middle of town, he knew almost as much as old Clyde, the liveryman, knew and Clyde had come to Tumbleweed almost twenty years earlier. He had come south to avoid the harsh, bitter-cold winters. Not only had he cut loose to be well south of cold country, his intention had been to also continue southward until every rime of ice was a memory, until he got back to hot sun territory.

They were both by nature and instinct south-west Texans. Carter, like most single rangemen, went north to work early and turned back southward when he felt the first hint of autumn.

The cowtown of Tumbleweed had little to keep its inhabitants from moving, but anything as upsetting as a couple of stage robberies was interesting.

After Bob Carter had made arrangements to bed down and his horse was fed and rested, he took advantage of what might remain of daylight to back-track that trail where the café-woman's husband's coach had gone off a cliff and where two stages had been stopped and robbed. He stopped several times until he arrived at where

10

those robberies had occurred, found the spot with little difficulty and rode a game trail down below where he left his horse tethered and scouted the area.

The stage was a ruin. He found where someone had salvaged three wheels, examined the splintered remains, found a Winchester with a bent barrel and a splintered stock, a scattering of bits and pieces and rode back to town with some type of an owl accompanying him part way. When he got back to his room, he turned up the lamp mantel and sat down to examine his findings.

Only one thing was interesting. Where the gun stock had been smashed there were two initials crudely carved.

He bedded down and was awakened by someone pounding on his hallway door with a pistol barrel.

There were three of them. Clyde, the liveryman, was in the centre of them and he was bobbing his head when he said, 'That's him!'

The other two were younger, had

cocked six-shooters in their fists and expressions that could have curdled milk. 'That him, Clyde?'

'It's him.'

'On your feet,' exclaimed the big, heavy man wearing the badge. He accompanied this command by leaning to grab a fistful of the stranger's bedding and giving it a wrench.

They also examined his weapons. As they left the building, Clyde hung back and half whispered to the stranger, 'Routine, mister. Come along with us.'

Not until they marched into the log jailhouse and a lamp was lighted did Carter get his first good look at the fat man wearing a badge. The lawman jerked his head and the prisoner sank down on a wall bench.

After he was seated, the sheriff jerked his head again and his deputies left. The last man out was the liveryman. His expression was troubled.

The bull-built lawman sat at a rickety desk, put the guns on it, shed his hat and leaned back. There was no mistaking his expression. He looked to be in his fifties, but it was hard to tell. His hands were as large as small hams and his gun-metal blue eyes neither blinked nor wavered.

He surprised the hell out of Bob Carter by offering a sack of Bull Durham smoking tobacco which the prisoner refused with a tight negative jerk of his head.

The lawman rolled and lighted a quirly, leaned back, trickled smoke and spoke through a fragrant haze. 'What'd you do with it?'

'Do with what?'

Sheriff Harney continued to trickle smoke, eyed his wall rack of carbines, pistols and rifles. As his attention swivelled back to his prisoner, he spoke again. 'Your name is Bob Carter?'

'It is. The liveryman told you.'

The larger and older man gave a scanty nod. He was one of those individuals whose stare went through a man without blinking. He sighed. 'Bob, you're in a way to be hanged. What did you do with it? I'm dog-assed tired. Pretty damned wore down. Me'n them others was ridin' on your trail until hell won't have it. Beside gettin' yourself hanged, I got a trade to offer you.' The large man sighed again, stubbed out his smoke and gently wagged his head.

'You think this over, Bob, they aren't goin' to hang you because I got somethin' else for you to do. You're goin' to jump off that bench an' make a break for it. You're goin' to jump me across the desk an' I'm goin' to miss my shot at you. Bob, it's late, an' like I said, I'm dog-assed tired. If anyone hears anythin' it'll be just one gunshot. I miss an' you're out the back door. By the time folks get their pants on . . . one shot, you're gone. But first you'n me got to work this out.'

Carter stared big-eyed at the sheriff. For awhile he sat on the bench in icy silence, but after a long wait he said, 'You're crazy. I'm not goin' to do any of this.'

The larger man shrugged thick

shoulders and smiled. 'Let me tell you the rest of it. You go out that back door. There'll be your horse waiting.'

Bob Carter's frown was the slow gathering kind as he sat without moving until he said, 'Let me do a little figurin'. You need me dead . . . you got this figured . . . you got something that needs hiding. Right?'

The sheriff nodded his head without taking his eyes off Carter.

Bob leaned back against the slab wall. 'An' those lads that brought me in with you have a hand in it?'

'We . . . no, not them, but that don't need to bother you. All you got to do is jump me. Someone saw you pokin' around where the stages were robbed. This way I can put an end to this without all the fuss of a trial an' such. Like I told you . . . there's a horse in the alley. You run for it.'

'Sheriff, that's the part I don't cotton to. Suppose you'n your friends just let me go?'

The sheriff very gently wagged his

head. He had been through this before and it always came out the same way. He said, 'Bob, I got a wife. I try to do what's right . . . for the town.'

Carter let go with a scornful sigh. 'You shoot an' miss me?' After nodding, the sheriff leaned forward at the desk. Where he had tossed his prisoner's six-gun, it was no more than eight or ten inches near the edge of the desk. His gaze was still fixed on his prisoner.

Bob Carter had seen that dead-fish stare before. In only one way was it likely that he might be capable of leaving this block-shaped jailhouse with its massive log walls and steel-barred windows and he did it. He launched his 145 pounds the same way a mountain lion of that heft went at a much larger, much heavier and dog-tired 220 pound dead serious sheriff.

He didn't reach for his six-gun on the table's edge so much as strike it with his body.

The gun caught in his britches as he and the larger man went across the desk, over the chair and down on to the floor where the prisoner caught a fistful of shirting in his left hand and swung with the right hand.

The sheriff made some kind of noise. To Bob Carter it sounded like the muffled cry of a turkey gobbler. He pulled back and struck again, this time without a sound emanating as the sheriff struggled falteringly to launch a strike of his own. He connected. But the big knotty fist slid along the downside of Carter's gullet while Carter's third blow was solid enough for the lawman to make a less fierce squawk as his body went limp.

Bob got a one-handed choke-hold and hauled back for the fourth time.

There was no need. The larger man went from sagging loose to plumb limp.

Bob Carter leaned off, waited several seconds before he leaned one shoulder into the big cocked fist and it went rubbery.

The prisoner groped, felt for a broken chair leg, gripped it with one hand and leaned back waiting to use it. There was still no need. The larger man was bleeding. It was difficult to find the reason, but, as Bob shoved off and pushed upright, a scuttling rat half the size of a cat made a noisy retreat, ducked into a floor-board hole and disappeared. Silence settled.

Bob retrieved his hat and his six-gun, used a blue bandanna to wipe his hands, and spared the unconscious big man one look before leaving the jailhouse by a doorway leading from a closet-sized storeroom and a second door which led out into a chilly dark night.

He was not surprised that no horse was waiting nor did he waste any time looking for one. He went down the back alley as far as the livery barn, found a nightman sleeping in the harness-room and, making as little noise as possible, led forth his own horse, rigged it in darkness, not for the first time, led it out back before turning it twice, mounting it and leaving the village riding slowly north-easterly, the same direction that had brought him here.

He held to that decent walk for over a mile before lifting over into a flat lope and holding to it for what he guessed was about a solid hour, then altered course and held to that direction until he had a little help from dawn light to find the small clearing he sought.

It was coldest before dawn. He shook into his rangeman's pelt-lined coat and stopped where he had meant to spend the night, before breaking a fresh trail which was still southerly but more to the east.

2

Getting Acquainted

The only country he knew was the territory he had crossed to reach Tumbleweed. There was no way to avoid leaving tracks, but if he could get far enough beyond the northerly mountains he would find flat country.

He remembered seeing an isolated set of buildings to the east about a day's ride from where he had spent his last night near that creek with the scolding nests of birds in some creek willows. He tried setting a course by sky-lining the highest peaks, a course which was not entirely satisfactory because as he had ridden south he hadn't watched which way he had come too well, but, as with most rangemen, he had an intuitive sense of direction.

He did not push his animal. In fact,

the buckskin horse had better intuition than its owner and with the night better than half spent the horse took him to the noisy little creek. It was too early for the birds to take up their scolding of intruders as Carter dismounted, hobbled the horse, didn't bother with the bedroll but took the bridle with him to creekside to make certain the horse would not drop down and roll with the saddle on. The loosened cinch was an invitation, but so was hunger. The buckskin went to grazing. If the urge to roll came to him, being hungry predominated. Beside every watercourse, grass grew in abundance. His animal hadn't eaten since yesterday about midday. It didn't raise its head from the grass not even after its owner dozed until the new day aroused the birds. After that, he couldn't have continued to sleep for the scolding he got from among the flourishing willows.

Sunlight made the difference. He could backtrack his trail without too much difficulty and rode easterly keeping to high ground until he topped out several sun-bright miles from that set of buildings below in a treeless meadow much lower down. He wasted no time admiring the beautiful setting of that hidden ranch, or homesteader's claim, whatever it was.

There were a few grazing cattle but not many. The distance was too great for him to know whether the animals were meat cattle or milk cattle. He went by logic and counted the distant specks. There were too many to be milk stock and not enough to be much of a cattle outfit.

It didn't matter, it wasn't likely he was being followed.

There was no downward trail. In that large meadowland below there appeared to be what Bob Carter mightily hoped was a pair of wagon ruts.

He angled along easterly sloping side hills until, when he looked back, the places he had ridden from looked respectably high.

When he got down where the tree

stumps outnumbered standing trees he found skid marks where felled timber had been cut, limbed and dragged in the direction of the buildings, and here he encountered a half-grown cub bear high enough in a bee tree that if it hadn't whined at sight of a horse and rider, it would not have occurred to the horsebacker to look up. The bear came down noisily and joined the horseman.

It had a shiny coat and a red collar, like a dog collar but larger.

His buckskin knew enough about bears to throw a fit at sight of them. Carter reined to a stop. The oversized cub came closer and whined. Carter sat a moment before wagging his head and squeezing the buckskin who willingly stepped out and for the remainder of the ride kept his right ear cocked. If the bear had growled instead of whining, the buckskin would have got a hump under the saddle and bucked. He'd been like that since Carter had acquired him a considerable length of time before.

The bear didn't crowd the rider. But three times when the rider would have cut downhill through brush and timber country, the bear stopped stone still, reared up and complained loudly before nosing for a scarcely discernible path and went down it a short distance before stopping to look back.

Carter smiled, shrugged and turned back to take the downward trail.

The bear stayed in front, whining to himself and occasionally looking back to be sure it was being followed.

The distance was steadily downslope for what seemed three or four miles before the trees and manzanita fell back and that large meadow replaced the rough country.

With a better sighting, Carter studied what was ahead.

The log house was more than a cabin. It looked to have three or four rooms. The logs were fairly weathered, several forest giants had been allowed to remain standing otherwise there were two small outbuildings also made of weathered logs.

Carter circled the structure from a distance to get some idea of what he was facing.

No dog barked, which was unusual. Every ranch he had ever come upon had at least one dog to minimize the intrusions of varmints, but this place was neither abandoned nor deserted. There were four saddle animals in a pole corral south of the house and they lined up like crows on a fence at sight of the oncoming rider.

A woman built like a lady wrestler emerged from a side door carrying a large basket of laundry which she draped from a sixty-foot lariat between trees which Carter had assumed on his approach was wet rawhide, to be stretched before being worked into a lass rope.

Her back was to the strange rider as she set about draping the wash to dry. She only stiffened and turned when one of the four horses, a horsing mare, raised her head and nickered.

The woman put both hands on her hips and stared. Carter reined and rode in the direction of a tie rack but did not dismount as he and the muscular female woman steadily regarded each other. It was customary for settled folks to make strangers welcome. Not this time.

The woman remained fixed in place like a cigar store Indian until the cub bear padded over to her and sat down like a dog to whimper. As she leaned to scratch its head, Carter said, 'I figured he had friends close by.'

The answer came back in a strong voice. 'It's a she not a he. Her name's Daisy. She was caught in a choke basket when she was very young . . . I suppose you have a name . . . '

There was no way to misjudge the burly woman. She did not look Spanish or Mexican and she certainly did not resemble an Indian.

Carter dismounted, looped the plaited rawhide reins and smiled. 'My name is

Bob Carter, ma'am. You won't likely believe this but I was supposed to be a girl. My mammy named me after her favourite aunt, Roberta. My pa had no use for my aunt. He shortened it to Robert.'

The large-boned woman muscled up like a Longhorn bull came close to smiling, up around the eyes, but lower down, in the area of the mouth, she looked as amiable as a scorpion. She said, 'You'll be a grub-line rider. They're always hungry.'

In fact, Carter was hungry. He offered a trade. 'I'll cut firewood for a feedin'.' The woman turned around. 'Out behind the corral. The axe is stuck in a round. I'll let you know when I'm ready to feed you.'

Carter had a question. 'All right if I put my horse in the barn?'

The woman was hoisting her empty basket and came straight up as though she'd been stung by a bee. 'No! Stay out'n the barn. Put your buckskin in the corral with the other horses.'

The woman went back to the house and entered by the same side door she had used earlier. She neither said another word to Carter nor looked at him.

Behind the barn, closer to the pole corral, he found enough log rounds to have come from several large trees.

His buckskin paired off with a horsing mare in the corral. A rawboned, tall, roman-nosed bay gelding took exception. Carter's animal ran him off with bared teeth and both ears pinned back.

The double-bitted axe was exactly where the woman said it would be and whoever had hit the fir round with it had half buried the steel. Carter got it free but sweated doing it.

He split wood, the sun climbed, a scent of cooking came from the house and the young she-bear either liked company or was not accustomed to strangers. She spent her time between a rear door of the house and the growing heap of split firewood where Carter worked.

He was strong, healthy as an ox, and in excellent condition for manual labour.

By the time his pile of split wood was taller than he was, his interest in the sturdily built log barn with its wide front and rear openings intrigued him. Carter was in his early forties and had worked his share of ranches, large and small outfits, and in all that time he had never seen a barn with two locked doors.

His curiosity increased right along with his hunger. By the time the woman hailed him from the house, the sun was lowering, the she-bear had eaten from a large pan made for washing clothes in and was sound asleep rolled into a ball near his wood pile.

He shed his shirt, washed at a stone trough, allowed the failing sun to dry him off, shrugged back into the shirt, lifted his hat long enough to run bent fingers through his hair and struck out for that same side door the woman had used. He had an idea it led into a kitchen and he was right. He was also surprised.

The woman was a good cook, plates and platters were mounded with food. She pointed to an empty chair and Carter dropped his hat and sat opposite a large, bearded man with the dark hair and eyes and the tinted complexion of some kind of 'breed.

He offered Carter no greeting, not even a nod. He ate using both hands. He had grey at the temples, and evidently used sticks to walk with, there was one on each side of his chair. During the meal he abruptly said, 'Name's Al Buckner. What's yours?'

'Bob Carter. Ma'am, you're a real fine cook.'

The 'breed-looking burly man stopped eating long enough to grin from ear to ear as he said, 'You'd ought to see her shoe a horse.'

Neither the woman nor Carter smiled. She refilled their coffee cups, looked at Carter and gruffly said, 'Look under the table if you're of a mind.'

Carter did not look; he said, 'Why, ma'am?'

'Because he's got splints on both legs. A green colt went end over end with him.'

Of the animals in the corral none had looked like colts to Carter but he said nothing. He smiled at the woman and went on eating. For a blessed fact she was one hell of a cook. About blacksmithing he made no comment. He had never seen a female woman blacksmith in his life.

The woman left the house using that side door. She wasn't gone long. When she returned, she and the man who'd said his name was Al Buckner, exchanged a look and the woman almost imperceptibly nodded her head as the man finished eating and pushed back his chair and with considerable care rolled and lighted a cigarette. He tossed the makings over in front of Carter who did as the other man had done. The woman cleared the table and snorted. Buckner winked at Carter.

'Don't like the smell,' he said, and Carter leaned as though to arise as he said, 'We can go outside.'

The woman turned on Carter. 'You can if you're of a mind. He can't. He's got a hole through one leg an' cracked bone or somethin' in the other knee. He uses them sticks to get around an' he ain't very good at it.'

Carter remained seated, knocked off ash and looked at the man across from him, then at the woman. Buckner's jaw set and his face coloured. Without another word, Buckner eased the chair back again, reached for his two sticks and hoisted himself. He was a strong individual. He jerked his head in the direction of the door and Carter arose.

The woman was solicitous, something Buckner seemed to Carter to resent.

Carter stood aside so Buckner could go out to the porch first and the woman shot him a venomous glare. She went back inside. Buckner could ease down into a chair with no difficulty. He called to the woman. 'Maggie! I left my makings on the table!'

She brought him his sack of tobacco and went back inside.

Buckner did as he'd done earlier, he rolled a quirly, fired it up and offered the makings to Carter who shook his head. He used tobacco but not often.

Buckner was more careful of the bandaged leg than he was of the splinted one which was too stiff to bend.

The 'breed-looking man said, 'That's quite a pile of wood you split.'

Carter turned his head as he answered and something licked his pant leg. Buckner smiled. 'Don't mind her. She thinks she's a people.'

Carter reached to tentatively scratch the bear's back. She stopped licking and leaned closer.

Buckner said, 'I told Maggie, she thinks she's a dog.'

Carter continued to scratch, as he said, 'I never saw a tame one before an' I was reachin' for my pistol when I saw the collar.'

Buckner nodded. 'Big for a yearling, ain't she?'

Carter did not know that much about bears but he nodded. He would have guessed her to be maybe two, three years old.

Buckner raised his voice again. 'Maggie! Come get your bear!'

The woman came, spoke to the animal and they both disappeared in the house. Buckner gave his head an annoyed shake and leaned back in the chair as Carter asked if the cattle he'd seen belonged to Buckner. Buckner ground out his smoke before answering. 'Well, sort of. They belong as much to Maggie an' her man as they do to me.' Buckner turned slightly in the chair. 'Me'n Maggie was goin' to mark the calves before I got hurt. Mister Carter can you spare a day or two? I can't do much but we got to mark them calves before they get too big to handle.'

The calves Carter had seen with their mammies on his ride down here were already too big. He said, 'It'll be a tussle, Mr Buckner. They're pretty good size already.'

Buckner denied nothing. 'What'd you say your first name is?'

'Bob.'

'Mine's Al.' The injured man called for Maggie again and when she appeared, drying her hands on a dish towel, he said, 'Well now, what do you believe of this? What we been hagglin' over the last few days . . . Bob here'll help work through them calves.'

Maggie stopped using the towel and looked at Carter. 'It'd sure be a help, Mr Carter.'

'Right glad to help, ma'am. My first name is Bob.'

She did not smile but she almost did. 'We're real obliged . . . Bob.' Her attention returned to the injured man. 'In the morning?'

Buckner shrugged. 'Suits me if it's all right with Bob.'

Carter was looking at the woman when he said, 'Do I bed down in the barn?'

She reacted as she had before when he mentioned the barn. 'No! You sleep in the house. You have a bedroll?'

Carter nodded. 'Yes'm.'

'Next to the stove in the kitchen,' she said crisply, and returned to the house where the men on the porch could hear her talking to the bear. Buckner made a disgusted sound and said, 'She went out huntin' berries an' come back with an abandoned cub bear no bigger'n a newborn dog.' Buckner clearly did not approve of anyone making a pet of a bear. Later, when Maggie told them she had prepared an early supper so they could retire early before a busy day tomorrow, Al Buckner jockeyed himself up out of the chair using his pair of improvised canes and led the way inside.

There was no sign of the bear until it made a whimpering sound outside the rear door.

Al Buckner let himself down very expertly to the chair as he said, 'Ralph'll be back in a day or two. Him'n them damned In'ians, and he won't like it you feedin' that bear in the house.'

Maggie answered brusquely. 'You leave him to me. Eat your supper an' bed down.'

When the woman went outside to quiet the big cub, Al leaned over the table and spoke in a lowered voice. 'Her man liked to have thrown a fit when she brought that cub home in her berry basket. He's got no use for bears.'

Carter spoke between mouthfuls. 'That critter'll really be big in another year or two.'

'Ralph'll shoot her,' Buckner stated. 'When she gets to horsing . . . Bob, you know anythin' about bears?'

'No, I surely don't, but if she's only a yearling I'd guess she's goin' to be awful big in another couple of years.'

Buckner swallowed hastily so he could repeat it. 'Ralph'll shoot her.'

Carter said nothing more on the subject of bears. When Maggie returned with the empty battered metal pan she used to feed her bear she glared at both men, but glared longest at the injured 'breed. As he positioned his canes to arise, he smiled at Maggie. 'Bob's right; you're one hell of a cook.'

She went as far as the porch door to hold it for Buckner. She said nothing, didn't even raise her eyes as the injured man passed. The look she put on Bob Carter was less venomous, but it was not friendly either.

As the men lit their quirlies off the same lucifer, they heard Maggie talking. As Al Buckner settled back to exhale, he said, 'She's real fond of that critter, but she'd better take it for a long walk an' come back without it.'

Carter went to pitch feed to the corralled animals from a shock of meadow hay that had been mounded outside of the barn. As he finished, drove the hay fork deep into the shock and walked past the barn, he paused to examine the large padlock on the rear barn door. As he was straightening up to continue his hike toward the house, his buckskin horse nickered from the corral. He was standing with the other horses. They had their heads down to eat. His horse had meadow hay sticking out on both sides of his mouth. He was looking past Carter in the direction of a three-sided blacksmithing shed.

Carter knew his horse. A grub-line rider doesn't own a horse from its green-broke age the way Carter knew his buckskin.

Carter spotted the stranger in the shed's shadow, loosened the tie-down thong over his shell-belted Colt and stood stone still.

3

A Long Sleep

He wasn't very tall, maybe a head shorter than Carter, but if a person added the length of the barrel of the six-gun he was holding as he cocked it, he would have easily been of an equal height with Bob Carter, or anyone else for that matter.

He was a rangeman from his sweatstained hat to his boots. He gave Carter time to make his draw and when Carter very carefully removed his hand from his belt-gun, the stranger smiled without any humour and spoke. 'You're smarter than you look, mister.'

Carter found his voice. 'Something you want?'

'You aren't him. What's your name an' don't give me John Jones.'

'Name's Bob Carter.'

'You work for 'em, do you, Mr Carter?'

'I was ridin' through. She fed me for splittin' fire-wood.'

'Is that a fact? Who's in the house?'

'The woman, Maggie, an' a crippled feller named Al Buckner.'

'Buckner's in there? Where's Ralph Conner?'

'All I can say is that there was talk of him showin' up in a day or two.'

The shorter man gently eased the hammer down on his six-gun and raised his hand. He stood silently studying Carter until a cock pheasant made a mating call over where the trees hadn't been cut. The stranger had made his decision. 'I'll take you back with me.'

'Mister, I came out here to do some chores; if I don't come back . . . '

That clearly had not occurred to the gunman, but for that matter neither had the appearance of the man Carter in front of him. He jerked his head sideways as he said, 'Unlock that door.'

Carter's response sounded valid. 'I

don't have no key . . . you mind tellin' me what this is about?'

Again the stranger took his time answering. 'I ask the questions an' you answer 'em. Who's the cripple feller in the house?'

'All I know is that his name's Al Buckner. The woman said he got pitched off a horse. He's got one leg busted and the other one injured in the knee.'

The newcomer finally relaxed. 'An' you're just a grub-line rider who rode in today?'

'That's right, except that I'm not a grub-liner. I spent the workin' season up north. Now I'm headin' south where it don't get so almighty cold for the winter. Mister, you got a name?'

The stranger glanced once swiftly over his shoulder then blew out a sigh. 'I got to take you back with me, Mr Carter.'

Bob Carter guessed the distance between them to be about eight or ten feet. Too far, he told himself. His adversary had drawn his gun with practised speed. He said, 'You're lookin' for the feller who lives here?'

The stranger nodded without speaking. He had a problem in front of him he hadn't expected. When next he spoke, the words came slower, almost tentatively. 'He's had time to get here.'

'Who?'

'Ralph Conner. He's ridin' one an' leadin' t'other one.'

Bob tried again. 'You got a name, mister?'

'Jack Tormey.'

'Jack, you got friends over yonder in the trees?'

Tormey's brows drew slightly closer to each other. 'I told you, I ask the questions an' you answer 'em. I want to see inside the barn.'

Carter shrugged. 'Can't help you. I expect Maggie or maybe Al Buckner's got a key.'

As the stranger took several steps backwards and studied the locked door, a woman's voice called from the house.

'Bob? Carter! What's takin' you so long?'

Jack Tormey looked at Carter. 'Answer her! Say you'll be along directly.'

That is the answer Carter gave her. Tormey made a crooked small smile. 'Pretty good. She'll figure you're in the outhouse.' Tormey made a slight hand motion as he said, 'Empty your holster.'

Carter dropped his six-gun.

'Good. Now move back, against the door.'

When Carter obeyed, the shorter man scooped up the pistol, moved back and shucked out the cartridges then tossed the gun back. 'Holster it, Mr Carter.'

After that second order had been obeyed, the gunman said, 'You sure there's no one else in the house but Buckner an' the woman?'

Carter nodded his head.

That cock pheasant crowed again. Carter looked in the direction of that noise then wagged his head at Jack Tormey. 'How long are we goin' to stand out here? They're goin' to wonder . . . '

Tormey had evidently made up his mind how he would handle this situation he had blundered into. He said, 'Bob, you're goin' to walk over to the house with me close behind you. Does Buckner wear his sidearm?'

As far as Carter knew he had not seen the crippled man touch his holstered pistol. And that is what he told his captor. Tormey still hesitated. If Carter had lied, his chance of getting killed increased. He told Carter to walk slowly and not to do anything that would compel the gunman to shoot him.

Carter read the gunman right. He was leery. He wasn't as nervous as Carter thought he would be if they traded places.

He tried a diversion. 'If you got friends over where that pheasant crowed you'd do better to get them over here. I got no idea what that woman'll think about me bein' out here so long.'

'You think I got friends over yonder?'

'Mister, I never in my life heard a wild pheasant crow after its perched for the night.'

Tormey blew out another long sigh. It would be quite a feather in his hat if he could capture the man he was after, if he could do it without help. If he could've brought it off with the man he was after in the house that would be even more of an accolade. He also wanted Buckner, but his primary objective was Ralph Conner.

Carter's nerve was steady. Too much time had elapsed for his original astonishment to have stayed with him. Carter said, 'Spit or close the window, Jack.'

The gunman's dilemma was acute. The man he wanted wasn't here and risking his life to get the less important man was not worth it.

While they stood in the increasingly chilly gloom they both heard the same sound at the same time.

It initially sounded like a solitary rider, but after a few moments it seemed to be two riders. They were a fair distance westerly.

Jack Tormey said, 'Aw, for Chris'sake, what are they doin' now!'

It wasn't a question and Tormey acted more disgusted than surprised.

Carter was listening in stiff silence. To him it could be Tormey's companions. He said, 'Your friends?'

The gunman did not reply; he was listening intently.

The riders abruptly stopped. Moments later someone yelled from the dark forest about where the cock pheasants had crowed.

'You got him, Jack? Jack? You hear me? You got him?'

Tormey's problem seemed to have compounded. He yelled back. 'I got another one out here. I never seen this one before.'

The answer was crisp. 'Bring him along.'

Tormey looked at Bob Carter and jerked his head. 'Start walkin', cowboy. I'll steer you from behind. Don't try somethin' clever. Just walk toward that feller's voice.'

Carter walked northerly and for several yards was quiet, until he saw what looked in the darkness to be several horses.

'Jack, how many friends you got?'

'Shut up an' walk!'

There were two of them, neither had shaved for a time and both wore belted weapons and carried Winchester saddle guns. Both men were nondescript in the darkness and would continue to look that way in daylight. They were neither young nor old and both seemed close to grinning when Tormey arrived behind Bob Carter. One of them lifted away Carter's six-shooter, satisfied it had been emptied, resettled it in Carter's holster. As he stepped back, the third man was visible behind him. He was tall, lean and badly in need of a shearing.

The tall man asked, 'Who are you?'

Jack Tormey answered. 'Grub-line rider. He said his name's Bob Carter. You ever see him before?'

'Never did,' the tall man replied. 'Grub-line rider? Mister Free-loader, are the folks at the house?'

'Two of 'em, a man and a woman.' As Carter spoke he moved up beside a high-headed, tall, bay horse who had thoroughbred showing in every line of him. He raised a hand to stroke the big animal's neck. One of his captors said, 'One hell of an animal, ain't he?'

Carter agreed. 'Sure is. I'd guess he could run a hole in the daylight.' His hand on the neck slid back to the hand-hold tuft of hair, he sprang high and was drumming with both heels before he got completely settled. The big bay horse gave a snort, jumped high and lit down running. He was a third of the way across the meadow in the direction of the house before someone back in the trees fired a handgun. It wasn't even a near miss.

They were past the house before more gunshots sounded and Carter had one moment to look leftward in time to see the light in the house go plumb dark.

Someone let go a shout which was followed by more shooting, but the big bay horse was sashaying beyond the house. The only control Carter had of his mount was the thick, coarse cotton shank he had been led by, but it worked. Whoever had broke this horse had done a thorough job of it. With no bit in his mouth, just the halter rope, the bay horse responded obediently to even the slightest pressure. Saddle or no saddle he was a pleasure to ride. When they got far enough southerly the horse ducked, dodged and sashayed among the trees and squaw brush with almost no reining by his rider.

The shooting stopped and when Carter had to slacken speed he heard pursuit coming in a dead run. He did not like to do it but he boosted the big bay horse over into a faster gait. It was

50

an excellent way for a man to break his neck, but of two choices this one at least had an outside chance of success, and while he hated abandoning his buckskin back yonder, he told himself that at the first opportunity he'd go back and get him.

The advantage was with Carter. He was a fair distance through the timber, shot out the southerly edge of it and came to that pair of wagon ruts which served as a road between the house back yonder and the outside world. He reined over to the road, slackened to 'blow' his brown gelding and listened. If the pursuers were back there he heard no sign of it.

The inside of his trouser legs were warmly wet with horse sweat otherwise the big running horse was not even breathing hard.

He remembered no buildings between the ones he had left and the village he had briefly seen, and without his saddle and bedroll he was feeling the cold. At a wild guess he thought the night was more than half spent. He wasn't particularly hungry, but he was tired to the bone.

This had been one of the longest days of his life.

He talked the big bay right up until he heard a rig easterly a fair distance. To his knowledge there was no road in that direction but to play safe he left the wagon ruts, entered the forest and stopped finally when he saw the canvas top of a wagon. There were two outriders, one on each side of the rig, plus a man on the box with a Winchester carbine.

If it was a bullion rig it surely did not look the part but whatever it was, with two guards whatever was inside was valuable to someone.

He waited out the wagon. When it was well past he turned back to resume his ride by way of the rutted trail.

He had no idea where he was, except that if he continued southerly he was going to fetch up in that place called Tumbleweed, which he had left before in somewhat of a hurry.

Where the ruts merged with the regular road he almost encountered six posse riders. He avoided a head-on meeting by going deeper in among the trees.

He watched them go by in a slow lope and speculated that they might be looking for the light wagon with its armed outriders.

He smelled the village before he saw it. Womenfolk were stirring their stumps firing up stoves for breakfast which reminded Carter that he hadn't eaten since early the night before.

He was right about firing up for breakfast, but until he saw flames to his left nearer the regular road, it did not occur to him what he smelled was from the roadside fire of some wagoneers.

He didn't hesitate. By watching the flickering flames he rode toward the fire, came into a coin-sized clearing where the fragrance was stronger and more tantalizing and was hailed by a knobby-kneed, half-grown youth with a double-barrelled shotgun. The lad hailed him which startled the bay. He shied, snorted and stopped stone still.

'Who are you?' the boy asked, 'An' what you doin' ridin' in the dark? Where's your saddle'n bridle?'

The boy's voice brought an unshorn man about the lad's height but three times as wide and thick. He pushed the scattergun aside and addressed the man on the horse with more civility.

'Evenin', neighbour. This here's my grandson Travis Morse. I'm Micah Morse.'

The barrel-built older man stood waiting.

Carter introduced himself, saw how the wagoneers were considering his lack of correct horse-straddling equipment so he said, 'This here horse don't belong to me. I run into some fellers trailin' him. I think they was horse-thieves. I jumped on him an' rode hard to get clear. As far as I know they didn't dog me this far. Mister, I'd pay you for a feedin'.'

The burly short man gestured. 'Is

that gun loaded, friend?'

Carter shook his head, lifted out his pistol and tossed it at the feet of the speaker, who didn't pick it up, he told the boy to do that as he said, 'Come along. As God's my witness, friend, it can't be said Micah Morse ever turned his back on a hungry human bein'.'

Carter dismounted. The older man handed back his six-gun butt first and smiled as he told the lad to lead Carter's horse off in the direction of the fire.

The third stranger had not left the fire, but he unwound up off the ground gnawing on a bone as he did so. Micah Morse said, 'This here is my widowed brother's boy, Roy Morse. Squat, friend, an' eat.'

Carter holstered his pistol, squatted and accepted the tin plate of food the other younger man handed him.

The boys were silent but Micah Morse wasn't. He was interested in the big horse. 'Thoroughbred, ain't he, Mr Carter?'

Bob stopped eating long enough to nod his head and say, 'All the way through, Mr Morse.'

The shorter and older man hunkered, reached in the fry pan for a slab of meat, drew a soiled sleeve across his mouth and spoke around what he bit into. 'Fast is he, Mr Carter?'

Bob Carter almost grinned. The bay horse was greased lightning, even weaving his way among big trees. 'Fast enough, Mr Morse.'

For a long moment there was silence as the Morses and Bob Carter ate.

There were two hobbled horses picking graze near where the little glade merged with timber. Morse pitched away his gnawed-clean bone and became expansive.

'You ever race him, Mr Carter?'

'Never did. Why?'

'Well, sir, me'n the boys moves around settin' up races while we head for Montana. Run out of workin' capital last spring. Mr Carter, you see that rawboned, leggy sorrel mare out yonder? She's fast but somehow along the way she met up with a stud horse . . . she's about three, four months along. She works fine in harness but she ain't fast no more . . . that's how come us to go broke.' The stocky man cleared his throat before reaching into the fry pan for more to eat. 'Mr Carter, come daylight let's us set up a run for fun between our mare an' your bay horse.'

Carter took his time before answering. 'Just for fun, because I barely got enough money on me to buy a bag of smokin' tobacco.'

Morse used a sleeve to wipe off with and smiled widely as he addressed one of the boys. 'Fetch Dolly in and give her that smidgin of rolled barley we been savin'.'

After the taller of the boys arose, scooped up a croaker sack that appeared to be empty and walked away from the fire, the elder Morse gestured toward the wagon. 'There's a horse blanket in the rig, Mr Carter. You can bed down next to the fire.'

Carter said, 'I'm obliged. I'm right obliged, Mr Morse.'

The shorter man leaned slightly as he asked a question. 'I hope you don't mind, friend, but I just plain never before come on to a man ridin' bareback without even his bedroll . . . '

Morse hadn't asked a personal question. That just plain wasn't done west of the Missouri River, but what he'd said could be interpreted as a question.

Carter's answer was delayed but honest. 'I took him from some fellers up country some distance. I think they was lawmen an' I think they was after the folks who live in that house . . . who got a tame she-bear.'

Morse was expressionless as he said, 'You don't say. The big bay's a stole horse?'

Carter hung fire again before answering. 'One of them jumped me behind the barn. There was a couple more hid out in the trees. They was careless'n I jumped on the bay horse an' lit out

. . . left my gatherings behind.'

'They come after you, did they?'

'I guess so but I lost 'em.'

'On that bay horse?'

'Yes.'

Morse sucked his teeth before speaking again. 'I'd guess the big bay can run, then.'

Carter nodded and made a curt nod of his head. 'Even in'n out among trees he can run.'

Morse arose as the other lad scuffed dirt on the fire as Morse went to the wagon's tailgate, groped inside, yanked out the heavy horse blanket and dropped it. He said, 'Sleep good, Mr Carter. We'll run our race sometime tomorrow.'

Carter walked out where the bay horse was cropping grass of which there wasn't very much. Other folks used the road and also used the little clearing.

The bay horse raised its head and softly nickered. Carter scratched his back and neck. The big horse put his head down and wiggled his upper lip with pleasure. He rolled his head sideways to gently nudge the two-legged creature.

When Carter would have walked away the bay horse nickered again and Carter looked back. The bay horse had been babied by someone, probably its former owner, and most likely a woman.

Carter returned to the smoking fire, rummaged for a treat for the horse, found nothing and, feeling the disappointment the horse had probably felt, rolled into the old, smelly horse blanket and slept.

4

A Companion

When Carter rolled out, the sun was high and climbing. The wagon, the horses that pulled it and the Morses were gone. Carter read the sign, found scraps near the fire's coals to eat, then struck out on the tracks which left the clearing bearing north.

It only occurred to him to examine his six-gun when he'd trotted several miles. The gun was unloaded which did not surprise him since it was unloaded when he had found their camp, but it was nevertheless a disappointment.

Where the wagon veered westerly and crossed a creek, Carter stopped long enough to wash and tank up, then splashed across the creek and picked up some dusty disturbances in the road but no sign of the wagon. He stayed with the tracks until the sun was slanting upwards and soon disappeared up a canyon. From where they entered the wide arroyo, he didn't have to follow ruts, just broken branches, saplings and flourishing underbrush which made it clear the wagoneers had to break trail as they went. That kind of travelling was mighty hard on the horses pulling the wagon.

Carter reached a place where boot prints showed how three people had rolled a heavy boulder out of the way. Here, too, one of the Morses had gone ahead on foot.

When Carter came to this place he studied the side hills. The westerly slope had timber, but where an avalanche had broken loose the trees and brush had been torn loose and carried downward.

It wasn't easy going; the ground was soft enough to be slippery but Carter started climbing.

He was satisfied the wagon had not been able to go much further.

He was about halfway up the side hill

before he altered course to follow the northerly slope until he was high enough to see the wagon and the three Morses.

They had worried their way beyond the place where the avalanche had almost entirely choked the canyon. Carter got among trees and sat down on an ancient deadfall.

The wagon was tipped on its left side. Ahead of it, the canyon was blocked where, sometime in years past, an even greater avalanche had closed off any further way northward.

The Morses were preparing dry twigs for a fire. Carter had to respect Micah's savvy. The lads were only gathering bone-dry wood which didn't smoke. Carter rested and watched. When they were cooking he could catch the scent. It reminded him that he hadn't eaten recently.

The sun was above the rim of the westerly ridge. He watched it. With an empty gun he had to await full darkness to sneak down there and get back the bay horse and anything else he could raid. One of the times he looked across the draw at the sun, he went stiff all over. Three men on horseback came to the verge of the opposite rim and sat there looking down where the wagon had lurched on to its side.

It required no vast deductive power to know those were the same men he had escaped back yonder.

How they had arrived over yonder in that canyon was anyone's guess. They hadn't tracked the wagon and men down below because they had come from the west.

Carter swore under his breath but recovered quickly. Now there would be five horses to be settled in when the Morses rolled in for the night. Carter needed one horse. His preference was by far the big bay breedy horse although he was in no position to be choosy.

Thirst bothered him as did hunger. He zigzagged as far down the slope as he dared. One advantage was that the further down he got the more dense the trees and underbrush seemed to flourish. Twice he tore his shirt and once a snap-back low fir limb hit him.

The riders across the arroyo disappeared. If the Morses had seen them they gave no sign of it. They were busy with their cooking fire. Once in a while a voice would reach Carter. The words were for the most part indistinguishable.

If there was a way down into the canyon from the north or west the riders might know about it, but neither Carter nor the Morses knew it or they wouldn't have turned up into the canyon from the south.

Carter had crossed a lot of open country, there was a chance that they had seen him when he left the creek back yonder and emerged tracking wagon ruts in plain sight and saw him enter the canyon. They knew he was after them and entering the overgrown arroyo had obviously been an act of desperation.

In fact, Carter thought, they did not know this country at all.

He might have had a boost in spirit if those lawmen, or whoever they were, had not come up on to the farside bluff, but if they saw the big bay running horse they might assume he was with the Morses.

Whatever the situation, Carter was satisfied he had never been in as bad a situation than he was right now — and with an empty gun.

He heard horsemen before he saw them, cursing as they worked their way up the canyons following the same wagon tracks Carter had followed.

The sun seemed to have been pegged in its position. The only change seemed to be in colour. What earlier had been a brilliant gold was now shading off toward a dusky, dark shade of red.

Carter inched down lower, utilizing shadows to conceal his movement. Someone, somewhere higher up the slope, or behind him, or angling to get higher, froze Carter in place.

That horseman had to have ridden up the westerly slope, in which case Carter would not have been able to see him. But whoever he was if he got higher as he angled westerly he would eventually see Carter's back.

Carter had to move, either upward to find the stalker or deeper among the trees parallel to his present point of vantage.

That choice had been made for him. With an unloaded six-gun he dared not go uphill to face the rider, so he selected a northerly route where the timber was thicker: it was his only option.

Down in the arroyo someone fired a gun and immediately Carter's world became endlessly and deeply quiet.

The noise and its echo created a deathly moment of stillness. Carter had a glimpse of reddish sunlight reflecting off a rifle barrel as someone with the wagon yanked his rifle barrel out of sight.

Morse was swearing. An uneven

spaced set of words sang out. 'You missed! Did he move? Where is the son of a bitch!'

The reply had a tight wound sound to it. 'I tell you, Uncle Micah, I didn't miss. There warn't no one there!'

The rest of the discussion was lost as the speakers lowered their voices.

Carter did not move until he had eyed his next position which left a slight open space he would have to cross. He waited. With no idea where that shooter had thought he had a target, for Bob Carter the wise action was no action so he hunkered and waited.

One of the younger Morses left the cooking fire, crawled over the tailgate of the wagon and returned carrying bed-rolls. They meant to bed down as they'd done the night before close to the coals.

A rifle would have settled the entire affair, if he'd had one. Even his six-shooter would have been usable, but getting down low enough to be in pistol range was not Carter's option.

He looked for that horseman, did not

find him and got into sprinting position. He could make the run without getting shot if the men at the supper fire would concentrate on eating. As long as he could see those three his chance of making it to the next, lower down, clump of timber and brush, before the men at supper saw motion and went for their weapons, might increase his chance of getting past the stalled wagon to where the horses were, get astride the big bay and get the hell out of the country.

Somewhere up the slope, a large animal stepped on a bone-dry twig. Carter flattened, twisted and scanned the slope above. There was neither noise nor movement.

This was another peril. How those riders had got east of the mouth of the canyon's mouth was anyone's guess.

Carter reconsidered his idea of getting downslope and northerly. He had a little more time. The sun was partially hidden beyond the rim of the opposite slope.

He was trying to figure a way to get northerly, to find a game trail he could use when the sun left. His empty six-gun caught a snag. When he freed it, the snag snapped back. It wasn't a loud noise but it indicated the snag was green wood.

He twisted on to his left side to scan where the shadows were puddling and looked directly into a cocked pistol which had the hammer at full cock.

The man recognized him as he was recognized in turn. The man put two fingers to his mouth. For some time they regarded each other before the man who had crept soundlessly down the side hill moved his hand and spoke.

'Don't move or make a sound. Carter, you damned fool. If you're after a horse you'd've done better to go back for your buckskin. That older man down there is Judd Mercer.'

Carter frowned. He'd never heard of anyone named Judd Mercer. The man with the cocked Colt made a good surmise. 'Don't know him, Carter?'

'Nope. All's I know is that the son of a bitch set me afoot.'

Carter recognized the man, but if he'd heard his name he could not recall it. The other man helped. 'The horse you run off on is Brown Billy — you never heard of him neither?'

'Never did. But if he's a race horse I'm not surprised.'

'A race horse? Carter, he's been winnin' races from Canada to Montana. If you'd just taken your buckskin . . . '

Carter remembered. The gunman's name was Jack Tormey. Carter's reply was short. 'My buckskin's as good a ropin' and herdin' animal as ever came down the line, but he couldn't catch a cold runnin'.' Carter squirmed until he was left comfortable then asked a question. 'Where are your friends, an' tell me somethin': are you a lawman?'

'Deputy US Marshal out of Boise, Idaho. I got dragooned to come over here an' help the local law to catch the son of a bitch who stole that race horse.'

'Where are your friends, Marshal?'

'Across the draw fixin' to get down into that big arroyo a half-mile or so northerly.'

Carter put his back to a tree and shook his head. 'They're cut off for goin' back or goin' ahead.'

The deputy federal marshal relaxed, but the cocked Colt did not waver. 'Carter, I had in mind endin' this before dark, but it don't look real good.'

Carter looked downslope where the Morses, or Mercers, were finishing their meal. He said drily, 'Well, Mr Marshal, you got maybe half an hour. After that it'll be dark. Look down there: it's already dark where they're havin' supper.'

Tormey did not take his eyes off Carter. 'Them boys up north will likely be down in that draw by now.'

Carter sighed. 'How'd you see me?'

Tormey's answer was curt. 'I didn't, my horse did.'

Carter plucked a spindly blade of grass and chewed. 'I'm goin' down there, Marshal. You can use that pistol, or come along with me.'

Tormey said nothing, but after a long moment of indecision he eased the hammer down on his six-gun. 'How?' he said.

'It's dark enough to commence sneakin' down through the timber if we're just a little careful. If I don't get killed I'm goin' to ride out of here on the big bay runnin' horse.'

Tormey seemed about to make a retort, checked himself and said, 'First, we got to get the horse.'

Carter sat up to look down where the fire was burning. As he was doing this he said, 'Marshal, stay behind me. I been lyin' here tracin' out the route down below. Half-hour ago I didn't see any way to do it, but the damned darkness helps. Put up that pistol.'

Tormey holstered his weapon and shook his head ruefully. This is not at all how he had expected this confrontation to end.

Carter was right, it was shadowy dark

and getting darker by the minute.

He led off in a crouched hike that increased or slackened depending on the available cover.

Where they eventually halted, the lawman said, 'Can you see 'em? What're they doin?'

'Keepin' close to the fire an' talkin'. Be quiet.'

For the first half a hundred yards, moving was not difficult. The brush obligingly thinned out. Someone swore with feeling and one of the others laughed as he said, 'I told you we'd ought to shoot him. Then we wouldn't be up this damned dead-end arroyo.'

Carter hesitated several times to avoid being snagged by one of the exposed roots of a tree. Tormey was careful, but the lower they got the more low-country trees grew and while he was watching the ground he put one foot forward into one of those natural traps and fell.

The men at the fire did not move nor make a sound, but Tormey did. In his threshing to free his booted foot he said, 'Son of a bitch!' but not loudly enough for the words to carry.

Carter turned back, hoisted the lawman, got him upright and pushed him roughly against the tree that had tripped him.

Without raising his voice, he said, 'You're goin' to get us killed. For Chris'sake watch where you're goin'!'

Tormey was too embarrassed to speak. He shoved clear and scanned the ground as Carter led off again.

They were within the last few rows of trees when a horse nickered northward and Tormey grabbed Carter's sleeve and leaned to say, 'That'll be the lads on the far side of where that damned landslide closed off the arroyo northerly.'

Carter halted, freed his arm, faced the deputy marshal and repeated what he'd said earlier but with more emphasis. 'Shut . . . up! Don't talk! You understand? Not a gawddamned word!'

Carter altered course; they went

northerly. Not only was the timber thicker and the underbrush less thick, but that nickering horse had been northward. They had to cross the skid trail where the avalanche had cleared a wide path and Carter wanted to approach the fire from north of the wagon.

Evidently this was different from what the deputy US marshal wanted to do because he raised a hand, but he let it hang there without speaking and followed Carter silently.

There was no way to avoid being seen when they scuffed dust to reach the far side and timber again but they made the crossing without difficulty.

On the far side, where they had to scramble among a mass of fallen timber and uprooted brush, Carter sank down on a rough old deadfall, wiped sweat off and told the lawman they should share cartridges.

Tormey drew his six-gun, shucked out three bullets and handed them to Carter, and as Carter loaded his empty gun Tormey said, 'I figured to shove some reloads in my belt last week; never remembered to do it an' — '

A wolf howl interrupted the lawman. He made no effort to complete the statement when Carter holstered his reloaded gun, stood up and brushed himself off as he jerked his head. They had to scramble over a pile of refuse left by the landslide to reach the far side and Tormey stopped to gesture. 'They got to be around here some-where,' he said, as Carter shook his head dolefully. There was no sign of the marshal's companions and Carter had not expected to see them. He was less disappointed than dog tired and thirsty enough to drink dry a modest lake.

Carter found a large boulder to sit on as he said, 'Marshal, sure as hell's hot your friends aren't here. I got no idea why an' right now it don't matter. We're to the far side of the dirt pile. We'll locate the damned wagon and go from there.'

Tormey's shirt was torn as was his

companion's shirt. They both also had bruises and it was several times as dark as it might have been when Carter arose, considered the scrambling he would have to do to reach the wagon, and started off.

His companion was no more gifted in reclimbing than he had been getting where they were, but with no choice, he followed the man he had allowed himself to be led this far. It was getting chilly which meant more discomfort. His rider's jacket was lashed behind the cantle of his horse which was tied to a tree back up on the rim where he'd left it.

It was impossible not to make noise as they climbed, pawed and grunted their way up the debris, reached the top, saw the tilted wagon and started down the slope without remembering their objective had been horses not horse-thieves.

If Carter minded the chill he did not mention it. He did not waste his breath talking at all.

The avalanche had piled refuse, brush, rocks, trees and brush as high as the average man was tall. To make the climbing more uncomfortable, the solid objects were so intermingled that reaching the top was not as exhausting as it was unpleasant. Every two feet forward resulted in one foot of back sliding.

When they reached the top in the midst of jumbled trees, rocks and brittle dead brush, Tormey's breath exploded in words.

'There's the gawddamned wagon.'

Carter turned, glared, and quietly said, 'You just plain got to talk don't you!'

5

A Female Woman

Men were talking and, while their voices were distinct, the wagon prevented Carter and his companion from seeing them. Tormey was close when he half-whispered, 'By the fire.'

Carter glared, offered no response and went down the near side of piled refuse. He stopped when they were within spitting distance to the wagon.

Two factors favoured them: there was no moon and the wagon's tilt hid them from the men around in front.

Micah said, 'We got to get the horses around here, rig some chain an' get them to snake the wagon back until we can turn it around.' He got no response. Carter and Tormey looked for shelter when they heard the men in front stand up and scuff dirt over their fire. Doing this, while it made good sense in a place where dead and dry tree limbs were scattered was advisable, it left the Morses temporarily blinded.

Carter counted on this as he started ahead on the tilted side of the wagon. The lawman followed being quiet until they reached the front where the wagon tongue was on the ground and two sets of harness had been carelessly thrown.

Carter drew and cocked his six-gun. For a matter of seconds, five men faced one another in the darkness, none of them seeming to be breathing.

Carter broke the stillness. 'Micah, you horse-stealing son of a bitch. I got a notion to hang you.'

Micah forced a smile. 'Well now, Mr Carter, we just borrowed the bay horse. Anyway, he don't belong to you any more'n he belongs to us.'

Marshal Tormey stepped closer. 'Shed your pistols. You young fellers, too. Now, damn you!'

All three men dropped their holstered Colts. One of them, young and frightened, erupted words. 'Mr Carter, we didn't mean to take your horse.'

Carter growled, 'Didn't you, now. Micah, go stand under that tree behind you.'

Micah didn't move, but the other young one did. He threw out both hands. 'He tol' you the gospel truth. We figured to borrow that big stout bay so's to help us get the wagon to where we can turn it around.'

Carter repeated his address to the older man. 'Go stand under that tree. *Move, you bastard!*'

The deputy US marshal spoke again. 'Not today, Carter. Not while I'm standin' here . . . '

Carter spoke without taking his gaze off Micah Morse. 'If you got a weak stomach, Marshal, walk out a ways an' turn your back. An' you, fetch a rope from the wagon.'

When the youth did not move, Carter levelled his six-gun and cocked it. 'Get the rope, boy.'

Micah made a sickly grin. 'He ain't

goin' to do it. Neither is the other one. Mister, use your gun or forget it.'

Carter put up the pistol looking steadily at the older man. Marshal Tormey turned abruptly, went to the wagon, rummaged until he'd found three Winchester carbines and walked back.

He did not say a word. He might have if a cock pheasant hadn't crowed southerly further down the arroyo and the marshal dropped the saddle guns, raised both hands and duplicated the same sound. As he lowered his hands, he addressed Carter. 'If you'd hung that feller we'd've had to take you back with us an' charge you with murder.'

Carter listened to men trampling undergrowth from the south. When the first man was in sight, the marshal raised his voice. 'North, I told you! Don't you know north from south! All right, keep your pistols on this crew while I go find her damned runnin' horse.'

The furthest back intruder held his

left hand high to show the lead shank he was holding. 'We got him, Marshal. About an hour ago. He was leadin' two other horses up out of here by way of a game trail.'

Carter walked toward the bay horse, ran a hand down his neck and lower, to the shoulder, ruffled the hair and smiled. 'It's him.'

One of the boys asked how Carter had known. He replied while still stroking the tall horse. 'He's got one of them MWX brands made with some-thing real thin, barely thicker'n a knife blade . . . on his shoulder.'

The youth retorted, 'Hell, mister, I cuffed him off from head to tail and didn't find no brand.'

Carter beckoned the youth, took his hand and ran it over the long hair. The boy leaned closer, parted the hair and straightened back as he said, 'I'll be damned . . . I never found that. Kind of fancy for a brand, ain't it?' Carter slapped the boy lightly on the shoulder. He was smiling when he said, 'They sometimes mark livestock like this. Don't make much of a scar.'

Micah growled, 'Tie him good, boy. Maybe the other two will stay close where they can see him.'

As the youth moved to obey, Carter edged him gently aside, took the rope in both hands and, with his back to the others, tied the horse. He then took the tall youth back where the others were standing.

Micah was tired, something that went with anxiety, long hours and no rest. He said he was going to get some more rope to tie the other horses which had of their own accord edged up to the tied big bay horse. No one paid much attention to him until he returned with a shotgun, both barrels cocked.

Carter glared at Tormey. Tormey shrugged as he said, 'I found three carbines, must have missed the shot-gun.'

'Looks like you did. Some marshal you are,' Carter said, still glaring.

Micah motioned for Carter, the

marshal and the marshal's men to drop their guns, then told the other two Morses to help tie their unwelcome visitors.

Each man was tethered to a tree. Micah was an old hand with ropes. When he was finished, one of Tormey's companions complained about being as hungry as a bear. Micah sneered. 'In the mornin',' he said, went to the wagon, dragged out his bedroll and flattened it near the tailgate where he had a good sighting of his prisoners, the fire and where his team horses were looking for grass over behind where he had tied Carter and the lawmen. He told the boys to keep the fire going and tomorrow they could sleep all day in the wagon when they got out of this consarned dead-end arroyo.

The boys did not argue. Evidently they'd kept watch other nights. One of them went scouting for deadfall dry wood while the other one got comfortable on the opposite side of the fire where he could see the tethered interlopers. He had his six-gun in his lap and rolled a smoke.

For Bob Carter time went past on leaden feet. Micah had tied with a double bowline knot. He could not bend far enough to reach the knot with his teeth so he stood head-hung until the boys were drowsing near the only heat. The night gradually lost its day-long warmth. The posse rider, who had whined about being hungry, evidently decided that if he wouldn't be fed and couldn't sleep he'd make it so that Micah couldn't sleep either.

He moaned, cursed, complained loudly until eventually one of the lads at the fire swore the noisy man to silence by giving an oath that if the lawman didn't shut up he would shoot the son of a bitch. The youth accompanied this announcement by raising his six-gun, cocking it and aiming it at the lawman's soft parts. The man stopped his racket. It hadn't awakened the old man anyway.

Tormey, tied next to Carter, hissed.

When Carter turned his head, Tormey whispered. 'I'm free.'

Carter's response was also a whisper. 'I wondered how long it'd take you to figure when he had me tie you that I knotted the rope with a slip knot.'

One of the boys at the fire turned toward the other lad. 'I can't stay awake.'

The answer he got was understanding. 'Go to sleep for awhile. I ain't real sleepy. I'll wake you up directly.'

Carter and the deputy marshal were still and quiet for almost a half-hour, then Carter said, 'He used a double bowline on me. See what you can do.'

The marshal did not reply, neither did he work the double knot free, he used a razor-sharp clasp knife to cut the rope with one downward lash.

Carter whispered, 'Guns,' and took several tentative steps away from his tree. The boy who was awake was methodically rolling a cigarette. His brother was flat out with his crumpled hat not allowing his head to touch the ground.

Carter nudged Tormey. 'Get a gun. The old man's got one under his blanket.'

For the second time, the federal officer did not accept advice; instead he started toward the smoker who was fully occupied creating a cigarette, a task requiring both hands. Evidently the boy was not an accomplished smoker; he rerolled his quirly to avoid having the bump in the centre as had happened with his first attempt.

Carter did not wait. He went straight toward Micah's bedroll. When he knelt and groped under the blanket for the gun, he was not the least bit gentle. Micah's eyes sprang wide open. He took in a shallow, noisy breath. He was looking into the barrel of his pistol in a rock-steady hand. Carter smiled and spoke very softly, 'Be still an' don't make a sound. You understand? Not a damned sound.'

Micah managed to huskily whisper his answer. 'I understand.'

Carter rolled Micah onto his side. He

did not want to see his face when he swung the pistol barrel. Micah went stiff as a rock for two seconds then collapsed loose all over. There was no blood, but the gun barrel had done the job.

Carter stood up looking around. One of the boys was doubled over, the other one sat like an Indian, cross-legged and unwavering.

Carter detoured on his way to the bay horse. He slapped Tormey lightly as they passed.

The bay horse had been watching. When Carter went to work untying him, the big horse turned, almost as though he knew what to do. He might have. Carter fashioned a squaw bridle out of the tie rope, sprang astride and kneed the horse. It picked its way. Tormey was untying his companions. He stopped long enough to watch Carter and the bay horse pass from sight southward on their way clear of the canyon.

Carter twisted once and raised his

right arm. Tormey returned the salute.

The big horse snorted just once. When they were back in open country, he veered in the direction of the road and went southward in an easy lope.

It was cold. It was also a wet-seeming dark night.

Carter knew they would reach the Tumbleweed settlement unless they changed course.

As late as it was, few folks in the town would be stirring. He was right. A bent-over older man was heading for a house from the milking shed. He raised his free hand. Carter returned the wave. The old man had a heavy, full milk bucket in his other hand.

The bay horse slackened to a jolting trot. He may have known what was coming because he only held that trot until they were passing the outskirts of town, then he broke over into that gentle lope again. He just barely made it. Saddle or no saddle, no one in their right mind rode a horse in a trot. There was an old rangeman's joke about that:

riding a horse in a trot guaranteed dead babies.

Carter did not really care in which direction he went as long as it wasn't back north. The bay horse had loose reins so he continued his rocking-chair lope until Carter hauled him back to his customary long-legged walk.

The sun was slow rising. There were blankets of dark clouds which were accompanied by the smell of rain. If the Morses tracked him they might be unable to do it when the rain came.

Several times when the horse favoured, Carter told him that as soon as he could he would shoe the horse. A tender-footed horse that favoured every time he stepped squarely on a rock would not be able to show speed when he had to. But, as far as Carter could tell, they were not being tracked.

Carter's hunger made him hesitate back there in that town where the eatery had shown no lights. He had covered several miles before he saw a lighted set of buildings off on his right.

The temptation to turn in was strong. If the house had been close enough to the road for cooking odours to have reached him, he would have. Some miles further along, another set of lights showed from a large house a fair distance from the road easterly.

The bay horse angled a few feet at a time toward that side of the road.

The sun brightened slightly past a rift in the clouds.

Carter let the horse angle. He presumed the horse favoured the berm at the road's edge where there might be fewer sharp-edged rocks.

Carter's idea was right, the big bay reached softer ground and he didn't favour, but he did something else that Carter thought was almost human: he turned in where that road led back to those distant buildings, slackened his gait to that long-legged walk and did not deviate.

A second light showed a yard or two from the larger building, and by the time the sun behind him shone in front he made out a large set of working corrals, some separate sheds one of which had three walls. The fourth position where there was no wall was a smithy. By the time Carter was close enough in the yard to verify what he'd thought, his mount was heading for that three-quartered building where he stopped and Carter laughed. It was not possible for the horse to realize he had stopped at a smithy because he badly needed shoeing.

The slit in the dark sky seemed to widen as Carter dismounted, looped his single rope rein at a snubbing post and walked back where he could see the road. There were no horsemen, not even a canvas-topped wagon as far as Carter could see in both directions.

A grizzled older man came up behind him. The tiedown had been yanked loose over his holstered Colt, but he was half-smiling when he spoke.

'Mornin' to you, mister. You waitin' for someone to come along?'

Carter turned slowly, not conscious

of his growth of whiskers, his torn and soiled pants and shirt.

He said, 'Good mornin' to you . . . mister. No. I'm not waitin' for anyone. Mister, me'n my horse is hungry. I don't suppose you'd give us somethin' to eat.'

The old man offered his rough, work-hardened hand. 'I expect that can be looked after. Mister . . . that your horse?'

The expression on the other man's face triggered some kind of warning. Carter hung fire before answering. 'Well, I rode him in here. By the way, my name's Bob Carter.'

The older man barely inclined his head. 'Does that horse have a name, friend?'

Carter was slow to answer again. 'I call him . . . bay horse. Why?'

'Because, friend, his name is Brown Billy. He was stole out of our barn some time back. Maybe a couple of weeks. You see his Mex brand? My boss's got two bills of sale, one in Mex, one in

English. Last we heard the fellers who stole him was goin' toward Canada.'

An unmistakable female voice called from the shaded porch that ran along the entire front of the large house.

'Ev, what is it?'

The answer was given without the older man turning. 'I ain't sure, ma'am. Maybe you'd better come an' see. This feller just rode in on Brown Billy.'

Although the distance was fair, both men could hear the woman's gasp before she started down off the porch.

The older man addressed Carter in a lowered voice. 'She's Pete Henry Morgan's widow. Emily Morgan. She put out the reward for the return of the horse.'

Carter wasn't surprised about the horse having been stolen. What surprised him was Emily Morgan who wore her hair like a boy, curly and close to her head. She wasn't pretty, but she was solidly built, in several ways not at all like a boy. He guessed her age to be in the neighbourhood of the late twenties. He was wrong: Emily Morgan was halfway through her thirties. She had violet-coloured eyes, had a wide, full mouth and a faint sprinkle of freckles in the area of her nose. She was wholesomely attractive, but not pretty, and when she addressed Carter her attitude was chilly. She asked where he'd gotten the big bay horse and before he could explain fully she fired another question at him.

'Don't you own a saddle an' bridle?'

The older man said, 'More'n likely a grub-line rider, ma'am.'

She looked Carter up and down before saying, 'Ev, stall Billy, fork him feed then come to the house.' She hesitated before moving her attention back to Carter.

'I was fixin' breakfast. If you're of a mind, come along.'

Ev looked from one of them to the other before walking back in the direction of the smithy to care for the bay horse.

Carter decided she was naturally

brusque as they went toward the porch where the house was as large as Carter had thought. It was furnished without regard to expense. The kitchen where she took him was not just large but fragrant with the aroma of fried eggs and coffee.

She told him where to sit and he obligingly sat while she moved an iron fry pan back over a burner. With her back to Carter she attended the stove and asked questions.

From the rear, except for hair, she could have passed for a man. A young one.

By the time she put a laden platter in front of Carter he had told the entire story from meeting the she-bear to arriving in her yard. He drank three cups of coffee in the process.

When he'd finished eating, she cocked her head a little and said, 'You knew I'd offered a reward for Brown Billy's return?'

He answered candidly. 'Not until your man out yonder told me. Until then I'd have swore that horse was stole up in Canada.'

She removed the plates, refilled his coffee cup and sat opposite him.

'Before you met those folks with the tame bear . . . you were going somewhere?'

He leaned back off the table looking steadily at her. 'I'm right obliged for the meal, ma'am, an' I didn't object tellin' you about what I been through since I got into this country . . . but before that I don't figure is any of your business, an' if you'd been a man I don't think you'd've asked.'

She showed perfect white teeth in a wide smile. She didn't take offence. She said, 'You met Everett. My husband hired him sixteen years ago. He pretty well ran things. We usually kept three riders. They quit last year; they heard of a gold strike down in Arizona somewhere. More coffee?'

'No thank you, ma'am.'

'Everett can't do it by himself. Are you a grub-line rider?'

'No, ma'am. I worked ranches up north. The first frost an' I started south.'

'Mr Carter, it gets seasonally cold here, but not like it gets up north . . . do you want a job?'

He felt the blush coming but had no idea why as he answered, 'You think I'm a horse-thief.'

Her smile diminished slightly. 'I'll take that chance. Right now I owe you three hundred dollars. That's for returning my race horse.'

'Ma'am, have you or your man tried to hire other fellers?'

'We've talked about it the last few months, but we haven't gone looking. Mr Carter . . . ?'

'Ma'am, those Morses'll be lookin' for me an' maybe those lawmen too.'

Her smile faded. She was dead serious when she replied, 'I have my horse back. You brought it back. As far as I'm concerned, if you had stolen him you wouldn't have brought him back.'

He understood that she wanted a

direct answer so he gave it to her. 'You pay regular wages?' She nodded. 'And found, ma'am?'

'Yes; you'll live in the bunkhouse with Ev. I don't think he's the best cook but I supply what he lists for me to get and I get it. Anything else?'

'No, ma'am,' Carter replied, as he pushed back the chair, stood up and made a parting remark. 'They'll come, ma'am. I'll hire on, but more'n likely I'll bring you some trouble. You'd ought to think about that.'

She said, 'I'll talk to Ev. Good thing it's settled. We've drunk all the coffee. Now I'll have to go into town and get twice as much as Ev told me yesterday we need. My husband's saddle's on the pole in the barn.'

She offered her hand. They shook man-style and Carter grinned. Over the years he'd heard men say they wouldn't work for a female woman. He never had, until today.

They went toward the barn where Everett was doing an excellent job of straddling a sewing horse in the harness-room sewing a saddle skirt where it had pulled loose of the sheep pelt.

Ev was a plain, no-nonsense individual, who had never been able to hide his moods. He smiled and gripped Carter's hand. Then it was done and he turned on the woman. 'You got my list?' When she nodded he added more. 'Might be a good idea to pick up four or five sets of shoes sizes six, eight an' maybe a coupla boxes of nails.'

She nodded, fished in a shirt pocket and wrote what the older man had said. She raised her eyes long enough to say, 'What size nails?'

'Same as always, Em. The big feller's tender. When you fetch back the doings I'll shoe him.'

Soberly she asked if Carter could shoe horses. When he nodded, she told the older man to show Carter around the smithy, and left them.

The older man took Carter to the stall where the big bay was dozing, full as a tick. He leaned on the bottom door when he said, 'You know anythin' about runnin' horses, Mr Carter?'

'No, an' the name is Bob. Do you run him?'

'He made a lot of money for her husband. He was a good man . . . when he was sober. I'll show you his outfit. You'll have to adjust the stirrups, he was taller'n you are. Come along.'

Pete Henry Morgan had indeed been tall. The two men went to work shortening the stirrup leathers to fit Carter then went to the bunkhouse where Ev fired up the stove for a meal.

As they talked, Everett ate and Carter staked out a lower bunk.

6

On The Trail

Between what Carter already knew and what Everett told him it wasn't hard to figure out that the running horse had been stolen three months earlier, taken to Canada where he had been raced. He was stolen again by the men Carter had encountered back at the foothill ranch. Clearly, the men who stole him this time intended to keep him for as long as they felt would be necessary for the furor of the theft to die down, then return him to Canada and enter him in more races.

Carter mentioned the locked barn back up yonder and Ev made a correct and shrewd guess.

'Them boys got a newfangled business; steal fast-runnin' horses, an' take 'em where they could be entered in races.' Ev had heard about the newcomers to the northerly country, mainly because of the tame bear. He didn't remember the name. When Carter mentioned it, Ev's face lightened up.

'That's it! A woman with a tame bear, a husband an' his partner. I don't have much memory for names any more. Em'll like to know.' Ev cleared his throat. 'I mean the Widow Morgan'll want to know. I been on the ranch so many years . . . an' we long ago got in the habit of callin' each other by first names. She's just plain Em to me . . . short for Emily.'

As they finished eating and the sun sank, Carter said, 'That's only half of it. A feller with two boys got the horse away from me. The same lawmen who was lookin' for the horse . . . they caught up. The old man got the drop on us. Me'n one of them lawmen got loose an' I jumped on your runnin' horse and ran for it. My guess is that they'll be along directly. He's not shod; he left tracks a blind man could follow down

105

here. Ev, I got to say I never figured he'd bring me back where he was stolen from.'

When Emily Morgan returned with the buggy-box full she stopped at the bunkhouse door for Ev and Bob Carter to help with the unloading.

The older man tired easily, but did his best at the off-loading and related what Carter had told her.

She followed them inside when the rig had been cleaned out and Ev fumbled with his hanging lantern until he got it lighted. She was hungry. Carter was surprised. Of all the cow outfits he had worked for, Emily Morgan was the first owner he had ever seen eat in a bunkhouse with the hired men.

They talked until late. She volunteered very little about herself but pumped Bob Carter for all he was worth. What impressed him was when she said she'd spoken to the deputy sheriff, a large man named Rory Hanlon, who had promised to relay everything she had said to the man who had taken the place of Sheriff Harney, Arch Cassidy. Sheriff Harney had suddenly resigned his job of sheriff, no reason given.

Before she left, she told them he and the sheriff would probably come calling in the morning, and she was right, except that by the time the sheriff made the ride and was taken to the main house it was close to midday.

Carter was brought to the main house where he met Deputy Rory Hanlon and his boss, Sheriff Arch Cassidy. Emily Morgan fed them before the lawmen left. When Carter got back to the bunkhouse, Everett was waiting. It was darker than the inside of a boot before Carter and the older man had hashed over everything that had been said at the main house.

He heard nothing until he opened his eyes to find Ev standing beside the bunk. Ev held a finger to his mouth and gestured. The night was not just silent it was also lighted by a sliver of a new moon.

Ev leaned down. 'Now she'll get a dawg. I been tellin' her for five years we need a watch dog. Get up, boy, get your pants on.' Ev was dressed and had a six-gun in his right hand.

As Carter rolled out, reaching for his britches, he kept his voice low as he asked what Ev was doing with his pistol in the middle of the damned night.

The older man whispered brusquely. 'They're out there. I heard the barn door drag.'

The old man pushed a pistol into Carter's hand. He said, 'It's loaded, Bob,' and went to the bunkhouse door. He exerted a little strength to open the door six inches and hissed over his shoulder. 'Door drags.'

Carter gestured for Ev to be quiet. Through the black darkness he heard a horse moving, not stamping in its stall, but taking steps as though it was being led. He eased around Ev, paused to whisper, 'Mind that gun,' and sidled past.

Ev waited until he could follow. As

with most ranches, none of the outbuildings, including the horse barn, were painted. Carter got outside, pressed flat along the outside wall waiting until his vision adjusted, then raised the six-gun and waited for whoever was in the horse barn to emerge.

He could hear a horse being led, but until it was clear of the barn he could not see a large dark silhouette.

He was ready for the confrontation when Ev missed his step at the door and came down hard on the ground.

The horse being led stopped moving. At the same moment, a man stifled a curse to the north of Carter where Ev had forgotten the bunkhouse floor was three or four inches higher than the outside ground.

Carter stood fast, gun poised. The next sound was of a man running back up through the barn toward the rear barn opening.

Carter went after him, ran past the bay horse who was frozen in place at the sight of a two-legged creature running past him.

Ev followed, caught the horse's halter and swung the big animal sideways for protection until he heard Carter and the horse-thief leave the barn running like deer.

There was one gunshot. Ev stalled the horse and slammed the latch down hard with the horse inside and flung around to join the pursuit.

A cloud drifted in front of the moon, with a result that made it difficult for Carter to see the fleeing wraith, until as he slackened off, he heard someone call. Then the sound of two horses hightailing it northward in the direction of the town of Tumbleweed.

Ev was sucking air when he stopped beside Carter. 'You see him?' Ev asked between breaths.

Carter did not answer. He was listening to the diminishing sound of two saddle animals going up the road like each one had a bobcat tied to his tail.

110

As they turned back, two lights appeared in the main house. When they reached the yard, Emily Morgan was out there with a double-barrelled shotgun. Ev began explaining before they were close. The woman grounded her weapon to lean on. 'Did you see him?' she asked.

Carter shook his head. 'Not real good. But I can tell you he can run like a deer.'

They went to the main house where she fired up the wood stove under a large, old, speckled-ware coffee pot. She had tied a heavy robe around her waist and didn't smile at either of them until Carter said, 'Young feller. Had to be. He out-ran me like I was snubbed to a post.'

They drank her coffee and returned to the bunkhouse. As they were inside, Ev said, 'Good thing you didn't shoot the bastard.'

Carter handed back the weapon Ev had pushed into his hand. 'Why?'

'Because the pistol ain't loaded. It's

got a busted firin' pin. I been goin' to fix it since it got broke last winter, but seems like I haven't had the time.'

Carter looked at the older man, shook his head, got out of his shirt, britches and boots and settled down under the bedding without another word.

Ev was a light sleeper. He spoke in the dark. 'Would that be the fellers you got the big bay from?'

Carter spoke without answering the question. 'The next time you do somethin' like that I'm goin' to slit your pouch an' pull your leg through it. Next time I'll grab the gun I came here with.'

Morning came with an overcast sky. Emily Morgan wanted Carter to ride into Tumbleweed with her. The sheriff wasn't there but his deputy listened to what they had to say and because he looked big enough to eat hay, Carter thought he probably didn't have sense enough to pour water out of his boots. He changed that opinion as they talked. Deputy Hanlon said something Carter had thought on the ride in.

It was going to rain and if it did there wouldn't be tracks to follow. Hanlon raised his hat, scratched and reset the hat before saying, 'We could maybe pick up their sign an' foller 'em, Mr Carter . . . if it don't rain.'

Emily spoke directly to the deputy sheriff. 'I've got things to do in town if you an' Bob want to see what you can find.' She smiled at them both and walked briskly across the road in the direction of the general store where the bald proprietor's eyebrows crawled upwards like a pair of caterpillars. She had been in his store just the day before.

Carter said he'd get the horse he'd ridden to town and the deputy agreed to go with him to the livery barn and get his horse.

They rode south from town studying sign. It was Hanlon who picked out the tracks of two horses being ridden hard northward.

They lost the sign on the outskirts of

Tumbleweed but quartered beyond town northward where Hanlon picked up the tracks again. All he said was, 'Ridin' slower now.'

Carter said nothing. He was an excellent sign reader, had in fact, scouted up redskin tomahawk raiders for the army some years back. He left it up to the man to follow out the tracks. One of the horses they were dogging had large feet and was barefoot. The other horse had been shod but not as expertly as a blacksmith would have done. Carter felt better as they rode down the tracks. The horse-thieves were going in the direction of that arroyo where their wagon had bogged down by the landslide.

When they came to the place where two barefoot horses and a shod horse left the stage road Carter drew rein, stood in his stirrups looking for the wagon and didn't see it but saw something almost as good: wagon ruts going from the arroyo southward until open country improved visibility. Carter led the deputy lawman away from the road.

He explained about the light wagon with its canvas top. Deputy Hanlon concentrated on reading the tracks and only commented when they stopped at a creek to water their horses. Hanlon swung one arm in an all-encompassing manner when he said, 'I don't see no wagon . . . nor any riders for that matter.'

Carter smiled, nodded and without an explanation resumed the way following the wagon ruts. He was right; the wagon marks were as clear as glass. They weren't deeply indented because the wagon hadn't been heavily loaded, but they were clearly the tracks leading from that arroyo.

Carter had a reason for saying nothing as they rode. There were shod-horse marks trailing the wagon ruts. He was perfectly satisfied who had made them: the three lawmen that he had seen last tied to trees back yonder.

Carter slackened to a steady walk

and right at this moment didn't care whether the deputy stayed with him or not.

Hanlon followed in silence. He might have been sulking but Carter hadn't pegged him as that kind. He had guessed the large deputy was a man who let off steam bluntly when he was expected to do something he thought could be wrong, and with fresh-day sunlight and miles of open country that canvas-topped light wagon should have been in sight. He nonetheless kept on the trail until they rode up an easterly slope and there it was, down the far side and moving steadily along.

Hanlon let go a noisy breath which was near as he came to saying he might have been wrong.

Carter didn't rub it in. He reined back down the near-side slope until someone watching from the tail-gate would not see them. He dismounted, looked at the deputy and smiled.

Hanlon reddened but remained silent until Carter made ready to mount up, then said, 'I'll guess they don't know the country. See them cattle on ahead? Well, this time of year the feller who owns all the country you can see to them far off mountains — his name's Greg Bekins — he runs more critters than anyone in the territory. Look close, Mr Carter, them cattle been bunched and drove.'

Carter sat his saddle with both hands on the horn with his eyes squinted nearly closed. 'Northerly, Deputy; there's riders.'

Hanlon who had been born and raised in this country did not look for riders; he raised his unoccupied hand to point far ahead where a sizeable clump of trees stood with unpainted buildings, a main house and the customary litter of functional outbuildings. Hanlon nodded. 'That's the home place.'

Carter was more interested in the white-topped wagon. It was threading its way between the ranch buildings and those riders.

There was no reason for the riders to

change course to intercept the wagon. They were aiming for those buildings. Some other time they might have caught up with the wagon out of curiosity but not this time.

It was large country with only one set of buildings as far as a man could see with the wagon rolling steadily well north of the riders and bypassing the buildings by what could have been a good mile.

With a climbing sun, distance could fool a person. The white-topped light wagon looked to be about the size of a pony and the sun was still climbing. Hanlon eventually said, 'Mister Carter, some day this country'll settle up but right now, as far a piece off as that wagon is, I'd say we won't overtake it before dark.'

Carter might have agreed, if a very distant, abrupt, sharp sound hadn't carried in the otherwise quiet distance. It was a gunshot.

The deputy came up in the bit like a hunting dog. Carter said, 'Looked to come from the wagon.'

Hanlon didn't think so. 'From the house, an' look at them riders pick up their gait.'

For a fact, the distant horsemen were riding toward the buildings in a mile-eating gallop.

Carter did not say it but it seemed to him the riders were closer to the buildings than the house and he and his companion were at least a mile behind.

He agreed with the deputy without saying so. He nodded his head and for a while he said nothing as he watched those hard-riding rangemen.

The deputy was faunching at the bit until Carter said, 'Those riders'll get there long before we can, an' anyway as far as I can see right now it's none of our business . . . we're after the wagon.'

But, despite his disclaimer, Carter's interest had been piqued. there was no visible reason for that gunshot; at least none that Carter could see.

They were well clear of the range riders and their home place and kept to the route they had started out on, even after the sun began to redden on its way behind some very distant and heat-hazed mountains.

Carter asked about towns or villages and Hanlon replied drily, 'Yonder south-east is a settlement called Tent Town. Used to be a railroad place when they were layin' track. Now it's mostly the centre for sodbusters, homesteaders, folks who bought railroad land. I haven't been over there in a couple of years. I expect by now they've replaced them soddies an' tents with wooden buildings.'

He was right. The only tents in use belonged to the most recent newcomers, and while natives continued to call it Tent Town out of ridicule, there was a solid log sign where the road made a sashay into town and out at the upper end.

The sign said 'Welcome To Free-town', but gave no population statistic.

Hanlon was tuckered as dusk settled. They could still see the wagon. The expectation was that it would stop for the night at Freetown. Carter would not have halted either if their horses were not dragging their feet and hiking along with hung heads. When Hanlon said something about being as hungry as a bitch wolf at whelping time, Carter smiled at him as they entered the village and said, 'The Morses don't sleep so I don't either. You can catch up come daylight or go back, Mr Hanlon.'

It was the kind of remark the rugged big deputy could take exception to and he did, but they left their animals to be grained and hayed at the liveryman's place, ate like horses at an eatery run by a black man, and walked out a ways to look for the wagon.

It hadn't stopped in Freetown and, as the day darkened, it was difficult to see it still going toward those far-off high mountains.

Hanlon shook his head. 'They got the telegraph up north an' among the towns southerly. This danged place don't even have decent coffee.'

As they went to look in on their horses, Hanlon asked if Carter had meant it back yonder about not lying over but keeping going.

The answer was simple. 'Keep goin', Deputy. That don't mean you have to.'

The deputy rolled his eyes skyward; no, he didn't have to, but this business was one of those things folks would know about and talk about until the cows came home.

Hanlon said, 'Now I been fed I'll keep goin'. My guess is that them horse-thieves'll bed down directly. Whether they can keep on goin' or not sure as hell their team's got to stop directly.'

Carter smiled to himself as the gloom of dusk gradually thickened. He owed those horse-thieves something and meant to pay them.

Hanlon didn't know it but he was riding with one of the most pig-headed individuals he would ever meet. There was also another reason for Carter to want to catch the Morses. He and the big bay horse had formed one of those feelings toward each other that occasionally happened with loners and their animals, and he didn't want them ever coming back to try for that horse again.

7

The Meeting

A few lights twinkled after the latest village had been left behind. Conversation between the pursuers was down to a minimum. Where they travelled over rocky ground, Carter dismounted and read sign from the ground leading his mount.

Hanlon was still puzzling over that gunshot they'd heard miles back. If there had been trouble back yonder they had ridden right through it without difficulty.

The wagon didn't climb when it reached the rugged hilly country up ahead, it turned off near a bosque of oaks and went northerly. Hanlon growled about that, got no reply even after the ground turned off rock hard and Carter had to dismount and lead his horse again.

Neither one of them owned a watch so Carter guessed time by the position of the moon, and after going north for what seemed to be maybe three or four miles the wagon ruts left the foothill country and sashayed north-westerly.

As Carter got back a-horseback he said, 'Damned if they aren't going toward that coach road where I first met 'em.'

He was correct, but the wagon did not take the road, it crossed it some miles north and rolled westerly.

Carter cursed under his breath. They were travelling fairly close to the direction where the woman lived who had the pet bear. He told Hanlon sure as hell the Morses weren't going to lie over at that place, and told the deputy about his experience. Hanlon made a prescient remark. 'If that's the place with the locked barn you don't expect they're goin' there to steal more horses, do you?'

Carter shrugged, which was not

noticeable without more moonlight than showed.

When he reached the log house and its surrounding yard where there should have been a light there was none.

He took the big young deputy with him. When they approached the porch and the yonder door, Carter got a surprise. The door was hanging open. He entered cautiously with Hanlon behind him. There was no sign of anyone and not only was the house cold but so was the stove. No one had been here for some time. With a curse, Carter led off in the direction of the bunkhouse. It too was empty; furthermore, bunks which had once had blankets had been stripped down to the liner, which was a long sack stuffed with horsehair.

Hanlon finished a big yawn and said, 'Now what, Mr Carter?'

Hanlon got no answer as Carter pushed past leading off in the direction of the locked log barn.

It wasn't locked, nor were there any

stalled horses, but there had been, the scrapings from feed boxes still had a hint of moisture from the tongues of horses licking up every bit of the grain the feed boxes had contained.

Outside, after searching the barn, even the loft, Carter stood in the night until his companion came up, then he said, 'You got the makings?'

Hanlon handed over half a limp sack of Durham with the cigarette papers attached.

While they were smoking, Carter went around to the corral which was empty. He growled, 'The sons of bitches even made off with my buckskin horse.'

Hanlon was about to speak, when an abrupt sound came from the northerly direction where the forest began and the cleared ground offered adequate visibility for Carter to see a man walking toward them.

The night-darkened shadow called out, 'Carter?'

Hanlon had his right fist around the

butt of his belt-gun when Carter answered, 'Tormey.'

The deputy marshal was close enough to be adequately visible before Hanlon released the grip on his holstered Colt.

Carter made an introduction. Neither the deputy sheriff nor the deputy federal marshal offered to shake hands. In fact, Tormey barely acknowledged the presence of Carter's badge-wearing companion. He concentrated on Bob Carter as he said, 'My partners are on the trail. How'd you happen to be here?'

Carter's response was an interruption. 'We can talk on the trail. Where are the folks from this place?'

'They're travellin' south. If you came by the road you should have met them.'

'We met no one. You sure they went south an' not north?'

'I'm sure. By the time we could back-track the sun was close to settin' yesterday. My deputies used daylight to find them people. They aren't travellin' fast, they're leadin' three stolen runnin' horses.'

'How about the feller with the injured leg?'

Tormey gave his head a slight wag. 'He's with 'em. That leg don't slow him down . . . with a hangrope waitin' for him.' Tormey paused when Hanlon expectorated in the palm of his hand, killed the lighted cigarette and dropped it before he addressed Hanlon. 'You after 'em, too?'

Hanlon ran a damp palm down the outside seam of his trousers when he answered. 'Yeah, but maybe like Mr Carter said, we can talk on the trail.'

The federal lawman made an irrelevant remark when he said,

'Deputy, if we catch up to 'em they'll be out of your county of jurisdiction.'

Hanlon snorted before saying, 'How far ahead, Mr Tormey?'

'By now I'd guess maybe half the distance they got to cover to get beyond your jurisdiction . . . unless those friends of mine have caught up with 'em.'

Carter asked, 'Your horse yonder in the trees?' And when the deputy US marshal nodded, Carter said, 'Get him. Ours are back in the barn.'

As Carter turned away toward the barn, Tormey looked after him, and Hanlon addressed him in a lowered voice, 'He don't eat nor sleep. Get your horse, friend.'

They came together, mounted and ready, mid-way between the barn and the forest, turned and with Tormey in the lead, left the cleared ground, got in among the trees and with Tormey busy ducking and dodging low limbs rode where tracks would be visible come daylight but that would be some hours yet.

When the timber thinned out, Carter got up beside Tormey and asked about the horses.

Tormey's retort was brusque; he was occupied with avoiding being knocked from his saddle by fir and pine limbs.

'They were gone when we got back here. I don't know what spooked 'em but they took those other stolen horses and lit out southward. For all we know they may be headin' for Mexico. They race horses down there so I'm told.'

Carter said no more. Tormey was as good a sign reader as anyone Carter had ever seen. Broken twigs, scuffed earth and the lack of wildlife were part of the federal officer's sign reading, even in the dark. But he still had to emulate Carter a few times before they got free of the timber.

Something bothered Hanlon, who had kept to himself after leaving the log buildings back yonder.

Where was the wagon? He got the answer north of the Freetown settlement when dawn arrived. A family of tent-town emigrants were climbing over it, children, adults, even a span of hunting dogs.

The canvas top had been turned loose of the bows. Carter surmised that whoever had been driving the wagon hadn't been experienced enough to avoid low limbs.

They spent less than a half-hour with the wagon. Getting clear of the people took time, but Tormey was brusque. When he flashed his deputy federal marshal's badge the people ganged together and were as quiet as mice until the riders left.

Tumbleweed was awake. In every small settlement Carter had ever been in, and that was quite a few, a company of strange horsemen passing would supply a source of gossip for a full month yet to come.

The riders they were following left plenty of sign. It seemed that every horse they rode had recently been shod, except for two large pudding-footed harness horses. Carter studied those tracks several times to be reassured they were following the right party.

They were.

When they got far enough southward to have the Morgan place in view, Emily Morgan's elderly *segundo* broke

132

loose in a high gallop, turned in at the trail to the building and drew up to a sliding halt at the house.

By the time the others were passing, Ev and his employer had been talking long enough for the woman to return Carter's high wave without making any attempt to join the posse.

Ev caught up a mile further along. He had an interesting story to tell.

A young boy had come from the north-east riding a lathered horse. Emily Morgan had fed him as she had done with Carter. He hadn't been talkative except to say his uncle would go off to the north-east with their wagon and he was to catch up after ascertaining that the bay horse was not close by.

Emily hadn't asked the lad how he would know anything about Brown Billy, hadn't even thought about that discrepancy until after the boy had eaten and fallen asleep in a chair.

Carter held a council where someone had lost a big shock of hay, probably off a cattle-feeding wagon. Their animals went after the hay as though they hadn't eaten recently.

Carter explained his thoughts. For whatever reason, old Morse had returned southward until he knew he would be the object of a search, then had made a miles-deep sashay heading back to the place where he knew about stolen running horses and a locked barn.

He had abandoned the wagon somewhere, not that it made much difference, and was now hightailing it toward Mexico on horseback.

A couple of miles further along, they encountered a homesteader waving some kind of towel and veered off to meet him.

He was young, unkempt and breathless. Before they stopped he started yelling. 'We got him in the house bleedin' like a stuck hawg. Come along.'

The distance was short and the spindly-legged squatter covered it in a flat-out run which slackened now and then as he yelled over his shoulder.

'Shot through the upper leg . . . maybe a day or so ago. Young feller, sickly an' won't say much. He was about two-thirds of the way to the house when he fell off'n the horse. Me'n my missus carried him the rest of the way. His name's . . . '

When the squatter seemed to hesitate as though he couldn't remember, Carter said, 'Morse?'

The settler's woman was waving the apron she wore with both hands. She was as plain and as agitated as her husband. As the horsemen swung off and followed the sodbuster inside, Carter recognized the pale, crudely bandaged younger man on the homemade bed of discarded scantling wood. It was the larger and older boy who had been with the wagon and the man he had said was his uncle.

The trousers which hadn't been washed in a very long time had been cut away to make room for the bandaging which was dirty, soggy red and makeshift.

The lad looked straight up at Carter, moistened his lips and spoke in a frog-croaking, unsteady voice. 'You, for Gawd's sake . . . stay away from me. My uncle'll be back . . . stay away!'

Carter blew out a loud sigh, asked the woman if she had some clean rags and some hot water.

She disappeared from bedside followed by her husband. Carter could hear them in the kitchen which only became quiet when the woman sent her man for an armload of firewood.

Carter's companions decided to take leave and keep on tracking, believing they could do nothing to help.

Carter said nothing as he rolled back the blanket and examined the soggy bandaging which seemed to have once been part of someone's old and patched work shirt. The lad flinched and gritted his teeth but said nothing.

Carter asked the lad three times who had shot him before he got an answer. 'Some damned cowboys day afore yestiddy when I was travellin' easterly between them an' some ranch buildings.'

Carter breathed through his mouth to avoid the smell as he dropped the soggy bandaging and stared at the bluish, very swollen, upper leg.

The sodbuster standing behind Carter, said, 'Went clean through.'

Carter nodded and moved to make room for the woman to put a kettle half full of hot water. The wounded lad said, 'We wasn't doin' nothin', just passin' along. I got no idea why he shot me.'

'Where were you?' Carter asked.

'I was drivin' when we seen 'em and I rousted up the team. I was leanin' far out on the left side. I heard the shot before the bullet hit me. I sat back an' hurrahed the team into a run. They didn't try to come after us, mister, for Chris'sake, that rag's stuck!'

Carter used the water to loosen the adhering scrap of cloth.

He asked the woman if she had any disinfectant powder. She did and went to get it, returning almost immediately. There were only three small rooms to the shack.

The squatter and his wife stood by in stony silence as Carter cleansed the injury, detached a scrap of dangling flesh, which earned a groan from the lad, liberally sprinkled disinfectant powder and had trouble where he had cut and prepared a clean bandage.

He didn't ask the squatter to get some whiskey, he told him to, and when the man brought it Carter told the lad to close his eyes, open his mouth and swallow. It almost didn't work, but the lad, accustomed to obeying, swallowed three times before locking his jaws and glaring. Carter smiled. 'Best I can do, boy. If the infection spreads you're more'n likely a goner.'

Carter stood up, considered the shellbelt and holstered Colt hanging from a wooden peg, lifted out the gun, shook his head at the onlookers, and quietly said, 'Boy, where is your uncle headin'?'

The lad wiped his eyes before considering Carter with a malevolent expression. 'South, lawman. South all the way to Messico. He'll be a-horseback the rest of the way an' you'll never find him.'

Carter sat back down. 'I'm not a lawman, Morse. Where's my buckskin horse?'

'My uncle's ridin' it.' The voice lightened slightly 'Tougher'n a boiled owl, that buckskin.'

Carter agreed. 'Yes he is. Did he figure to race that big bay in Mexico?'

The lad nodded. His jaws were locked against pain.

The squatter woman tapped Carter's shoulder. 'Is he an outlaw, mister?'

'Yes'm. Him, his uncle an' another one. This one's brother, I think.'

The man had a more practical question to ask. 'Well, what'll we do with him?'

Carter smiled. 'Break him to lead for all I care. Set him to plantin' for you. Except for his outlaw, horse-stealin' uncle I don't expect he's got any kin. How about it, young feller?'

The lad nodded again without speaking until Carter arose, emptied the lad's six-gun on the floor and handed the weapon to the squatter. 'Keep an eye on him, friend. Don't let him get that gun an' reload it. I don't think the other two'll come back for him but just in case, keep a close watch. They work best at night. Ma'am, I'll thank you for him. I don't think he knows how to say thanks. Ma'am, if you got something edible . . . ?'

He followed the woman to her kitchen where she wordlessly made up a bundle of food and gave it to Carter as she said, 'If he makes it, Mister . . . '

'Carter, ma'am.'

'If he makes it, Mr Carter, he'll owe it to you, not us. We're right obliged. If you're ever back this way . . . '

He smiled, accepted the bundle and left with a hot sun climbing. There wasn't even any dust to indicate where the riders he had been with could be.

He considered continuing on southward but he was riding someone else's horse and if he was apprehended this time, as sure as roses smell they'd hang him for horse-theft.

He decided to ride north as far as the Tumbleweed settlement. He was probably wanted there, but at least it did not seem very likely that he would be recognized. Mostly his activity in the Tumbleweed community had occurred after dark.

He had another reason. He was less concerned with being recognized than he was in recovering his buckskin horse. He rode without haste back the way he had come with dust rising in the wake of a southbound stage, the only traffic he could see as the heat increased in an expanse of open country bordered in all directions by forested uplands.

He didn't get there. Not this time. Emily Morgan was riding out of her private road to where it junctured with the stage road. He might have eluded her if he'd seen her in time, but he hadn't so when they met Carter removed his hat and smiled.

She smiled back. 'If you're going to town we might as well ride together,' she said, and reined in beside him going north.

It was a pleasant ride. They talked. She told him how much Brown Billy had been worth through his winnings to herself and her late husband. In turn, Carter told her of his adventures since arriving at the northerly ranch where the woman kept a tame bear. Quite a number of local people knew about it. The cowmen had formed a group dedicated to shooting the bear on sight. Wild bears lived off livestock. A bear that did not fear people would be considered even more of a hazard.

When they reached Tumbleweed, Emily Morgan hailed a large, balding man wearing a sheriff's badge as he was leaving an eatery with a toothpick in his mouth. He said his deputy wasn't in town and hadn't left a note about his absence.

They discussed horse-thieves in general and her loss in particular. Carter wondered why the woman didn't mention that her running horse had been recovered.

Later, at a café, he asked her about that and she replied in a voice of almost indifference.

'I waited for him to say something. When he didn't I decided not to tell him.'

Her answer left Carter wondering in silence how she reasoned. His thoughts were scattered when three stockmen came into the café and immediately got a conversation going with Emily Morgan. They were concerned about the theft of her running horse.

Carter acknowledged each introduction to the ranchers and went to work on his meal while avoiding implication in the conversations, but he was intrigued how the woman sidestepped direct answers concerning her stolen race horse.

When they finished eating and went down to the general store Carter finally asked her point blank why she had not told the cowmen her horse had been recovered and her answer explained something Carter knew nothing about.

She stopped beneath the shading overhang in front of the emporium, looked Carter in the face and said, 'I don't like gossip, Bob, and those three are worse than their wives for being gossips.'

He followed her into the store in silence. Her answer had seemed to imply something else and he could not make sense of it.

Tom Leary, the storekeeper, smiled at the woman and nodded his recognition of the rangeman with her before he said, 'My boy that takes care of outlying deliveries come across your hired man ridin' with some other fellers miles north of here. Are they lookin' for strays, ma'am?'

Emily smiled at the storekeeper and nodded her head. 'Most likely, Tom.

You knew horse-thieves raided me some time back. Well, if it's true trouble comes in twos why then I most likely been hit by cattle-rustlers too.'

She handed the storekeeper a slip of paper. 'If you'll fill this order I'll be back for it directly.'

Leary took the list, read it twice and nodded. He would do exactly as she requested.

Carter was outside under the over-hang, when he said, 'Ma'am, I'd take it kindly if you'd explain something to me.'

She smiled which made her prettier and younger than she was when she replied, 'About the race horse?'

'Well,' he said, 'that too. You didn't answer them cowmen straight out.'

'The reason,' she told him, 'is simple, Bob. The horse is insured for three thousand dollars. Insurance companies only pay if the horse is dead.' She paused watching his expression lighten as he understood; then she spoke again, in a softer and quieter tone this time. 'By the time I'd paid my dead husband's debts I was almost broke. If the horse is never found and is presumed to be dead I'll get the three thousand dollars and I'll be able to carry on until next Fall when I sell off the cattle ready for market. Bob . . . ?'

'Yes, ma'am.'

'I don't know why I told you this . . . if you tell Ev or anyone else . . . '

Carter looked across the road where the sheriff and one of those cowmen who had been at the café were talking.

She said, 'Bob!' in a not quite steady voice.

He answered. 'I just work for you, ma'am. I got no interest in your private affairs.'

They got her purchases from the store and headed south. Before Carter could make out her ranch buildings, she said, 'It's dishonest, isn't it?'

He hung fire before answering. 'Well, like I said, it's none of my business, but for that kind of money they just might send someone out here to make sure the horse is really dead.'

She smiled over at him. 'He won't be here.'

Carter nodded slightly. He'd heard from older men that female women could be as deceptive as the weather. His own experience with them had been limited. He'd been married once, for eleven years. He'd had a son. He'd also had all he could stomach of the woman and had left. Later, he'd heard his wife had died and he returned, placing his son in the care of his wife's brother.

When they reached the turnoff leading to her buildings she raised her reins to take the private road. When Bob Carter did not follow, she stopped, looked long at him and said, 'Ride in with me.'

He made a small smile and shook his head. 'I'll catch up with those posse-men. But to do that I'll have to take your bay horse.'

He raised his hat to her, headed to the barn, saddling Brown Billy and rode onward without haste until he'd covered a fair distance then boosted the horse over into a lope and maintained that gait until the ranch buildings behind him were distant enough to appear very small.

8

Cornered

The flat country gradually became broken and uneven. He watched to his left as he passed along and eventually saw what he was watching for: an area where the road made a series of snake-like curves and bends following territory which had fewer lifts and falls, then sashayed in a sidelong miles-deep line southward to avoid climbing an area of rugged broken country.

Carter left the road, followed arroyos, climbing only when he had to and when there was no alternative, to a high knob and traced out by sight how the road made a north-easterly conclusion of its immense curve to finally resume its way hugging the foothills. He smiled, told his horse the moving specks raising distant dust would be the band of riders he had abandoned miles back.

It was hard country. Whoever had pioneered that road had chosen the best way to reach his destination with a minimum of climbing, particularly stage and wagon traffic.

His route, rough and cluttered, would cut off several miles before it returned to the flat, passable foothill country.

The last time he climbed where he could top-out with a view of the coach road, he could see the posse riders below and to the rear of his vantage point.

It only marginally worried him that those riders far below would see him and after he left the top-out to pick his way downhill where he would eventually come to the coach road, the day had passed into afternoon.

He wanted to meet the other riders. To accomplish this he took his time working his way so that when he emerged within pistol shot of the road he would achieve a juncture.

His mount was sweaty and scratched from having to force its way through stands of thorny undergrowth.

Where he emerged on to the road and halted to rest his animal he could distantly see the riders coming but could not hear them.

He tied his horse in the shade of an ancient oak tree whose limbs had once been trimmed so as not to interfere with laden wagons on the road.

He knew where the road started, on the far north side of the distant, heat-hazed northerly mountains which he had crossed days earlier, but where it ended was anyone's guess and where Carter sat on a warm boulder to wait, there was evidence that the road had not been used often.

He was unaware that he had made a mistake in the little lay-by where he and his horse were resting. The riders he was awaiting had to be several miles back. The older man who had abandoned his wagon was up ahead, close enough in the lead to have seen Carter come out of an arroyo.

He did not think of the man who was being pursued, until up ahead around a bend in the road, a roaming band of wild mountain sheep made a racket as they too came out into the road bleating and running as though their lives depended on it.

Carter arose, walked out onto the road looking easterly where the mountain sheep ran in pure abandon.

Carter returned to his tree shade, found his boulder and sat down again when the voice he recognized spoke from behind and easterly, the only sound for miles in all directions.

'Mister, you so much as sneeze an' I'll blow your damned head off!'

Carter didn't sneeze. He didn't even sigh, but he very slowly twisted from the middle.

Morse's shirt was torn, there was blood where thorns had caught him. His face was sweat-shiny, but the fist holding the cocked six-gun was as steady as stone.

Carter was too surprised to speak but Morse wasn't. 'Mister, one or t'other of us is bad for the other one. I was watching that herd of riders from up yonder. I could have left them miles back if that damned buckskin horse hadn't come up lame.'

That was Carter's second surprise. His buckskin horse had never known a lame day in his life; at least not since Carter had owned him.

Morse wasn't finished. 'I got to take your animal an' I got to do it soon, them fellers back yonder'll catch up soon. You stand up an' shed your sidearm.'

Carter arose slowly, turning as he did so. When they were facing each other, the older man spat aside before speaking again.

'Cat got your tongue? Stand clear of where you was sittin'.'

Again Carter obeyed. When the distance between them was adequate, Morse leathered his pistol and forced an unpleasant smile. 'You tell them lads when they get up here I took the horse and headed south, straight south.'

Carter did not move until Morse was moving in the direction of his tethered horse then he leaned down soundlessly, reached for a stone and was straightening when Morse turned back, right hand inches from his holstered weapon.

Carter hurled the stone. It went wide of its mark but it made Morse flinch, jump sideways and go for his Colt. He bumped his hand before he could bring the gun to bear after Carter knocked him off balance. Morse fired, missed by twelve inches and Carter was on him, fists pumping.

Morse was tough, he absorbed blows and rolled, trying to get another shot. Something behind him and above made a frightened bleat and kicked loose pieces of shale which rained down. One, a sliver of blue greyish stone hit Morse between the shoulders. He was scrambling to his feet and swung his head. Carter caught him under the right ear with a desperate strike. Morse wrenched to face back around and his eyes widened as he crumpled forward.

Carter wasted no time. He grabbed the six-gun, shoved the inert horse-thief with his foot, reached for the tethered reins, swung the horse toward him and leapt. He came down in the saddle with the horse already moving.

Further back, someone fired a pistol. The range was too great. As Carter swept around the long-spending curve in the old road, he saw his buckskin horse. He had known that animal a long time and while it had bottom enough to outlast pursuit it was not fast. He stopped long enough to set the buckskin free, loop the reins under and over the gullet end around the horn, with plenty of slack, then got back astride and kneed his mount into a run. The buckskin followed, favouring one front leg and losing ground but did the best he could do.

Carter rode looking back and failed to see the herd of off-breed cattle being driven directly toward him.

He had a moment to decide on a course. If he reined easterly, the road fell away toward rock ledges; if he reined in the opposite direction, he would have to climb upwards over a bed of loose rock.

He dismounted on the fly, holding one rein and cocked his six-gun.

The first man to come around the bend was that potgutted big ex-sheriff from Tumbleweed.

Carter fired high. In a place boxed in on both sides the sheriff faced the same problem Carter had faced, except that ex-Sheriff Harney did not climb the slope nor go over the drop-off, he slammed to a halt, fired at Carter's rock and dismounted, yelling for his companions to go up and around where they could come down behind Carter.

Not a single one of them moved to obey. Carter fired off two more rounds before those driven cattle behind him stopped in their tracks and someone far back, who was a drover, yelled furiously and rode into the driven critters.

Some of the cattle tried to squeeze around on the upper side and made it. Others followed. Carter's mount faunched and would have swung around and raced for it, if the rider further back hadn't fired into the air and yelled. The riders saw the cattle coming toward them and tried to rein clear. They made it, but terrified cattle ran blind. They barrelled into the possemen knocking at least two horses to their knees.

Carter yanked the reins, got his animal close enough and vaulted into the saddle. Carter was nearly engulfed by driven cattle which mostly had horns, but by the time he could see two riders doing the driving he was almost clear. A youth in about his mid-teens swung his horse sideways to block the road and held a cocked six-gun high as he yelled 'Stop! Stop right where you are, mister. *Stop*!'

The distance between them was no more than six or eight feet. Carter had no intention of stopping. He flashed his left hand downward for the holstered weapon he had picked up back yonder from Morse . . . at that moment a large brockle-faced cow, young and fat, barrelled into his horse. It went down in an awkward sprawl.

Carter tried to roll, but a second animal stumbled over him, fell to its knees, bawled in distress, got back upright and went in pursuit of its companions.

Carter's attempt to roll clear brought him in contact with a boulder the size of a melon.

By the time he regained consciousness, the cattle were bolting around the bend and someone needing a shave and a shearing had his head and shoulder off the ground using one bent knee to keep Carter off the ground.

There was blood on the left side of his face and it was also matting in his hair. He felt himself being lifted by the ankles and the shoulders. He was carried to the uphill side of the road when someone fired a pistol. He fumbled awkwardly, but his holster was empty and the man standing over him spoke in a gruff, gravelly voice.

'Mister, you're lucky you didn't get knocked down at the head of the drive.' The unshaven individual drew forth a folded, clean, blue bandanna and dropped it on Carter. 'Wipe off the blood.'

Carter was thoroughly baffled. The cattle had gone around the bend where the gunshot had sounded. One of the men had fired off a round to divert the herd. Carter couldn't determine whether that ruse had worked or not; there was a thick cloud of dust but no cattle in sight.

A second drover came back and the man standing with Carter said, 'Aggie, I'll hoist him up over your saddle. He don't know up from down. Take him home.'

Carter heard the reply and the voice belonged to a woman. 'There's a band of 'em run into the cattle near the turnoff.'

The man answered with no hesitation. 'Take him home, girl! I'll take care of his friends. Now, hold that horse still.'

Carter felt powerful arms shoved under him. He was lifted as though he was weightless, carried a few steps and eased down on saddle leather.

He said it again. 'Go, girl!'

'What about them fellers back yonder?'

'Dammit, girl, go! Keep hold so he don't slide off. *Go!*'

Of all the ways to ride a horse being belly-down was the worst. Carter's head cleared as he was carried away in a racking gallop. On the far left side he could feel tie-thongs and gripped them but on the other side where his feet and legs were there was no way to do anything but balance and when the ridden horse abruptly veered left he had all he could do to keep from going off head first.

The rider scolded him and used one hand to help him stay athwart, holding her reins and the reins of the horse Carter was belly down on.

The horses slackened to a rough trot when Carter was sure he was going to lose consciousness again.

The woman said, 'That's right . . . balance . . . you're too big for me to do it all.'

Carter thought he heard gunshots. They sounded distant but he wasn't sure. He didn't lose consciousness, but only because when the woman set up her mount and released her grip he went head first off on the left side. The horse shied a few feet and looked around. The woman dismounted, yelled for someone named Maude to take the horses and leaned to help Carter sit up.

She took the cloth her father had dropped and wiped off the blood. A second woman appeared. This one was older, stocky and wore her grey hair almost as short as a man's.

They exchanged few words before the horses were led away. Carter, supported by a strong leg, took the cloth to continue wiping off with it as he forced himself to gradually hoist himself into a sitting position.

She blushed. 'I'm Agnes. I think you'll be a man named Carter . . . a horse-thief.'

His smile faded. 'I'm Carter, ma'am, but I'm not a horse-thief.'

'Aren't you? You were riding the Morgans' running horse. We know that horse. Everyone in the country round-about knows him. They wouldn't sell him.'

The aproned older woman returned from looking after the horses. She ignored Carter when she addressed the girl. 'Where's your pa?'

The girl explained; the older woman listened until she caught sight of a rider with a buckskin horse trailing behind. She quietly said, 'That man's goin' to give me a full head of white hair.' She went over to meet the man who dismounted and led the horses the rest of the way with the woman scolding him for all she was worth.

Carter stood up. As the older man passed, he tossed Carter a pistol but did not stop. The older woman did not let up even after she and her husband were in a barn made of adobe halfway up and peeled logs the rest of the way. A pole corral nearby had its gate sagging wide open.

Carter told the girl he had no idea anyone lived in this territory, he thought it all belonged to Emily Morgan.

The girl's lip drew into a flat line. 'We adjoin,' she said somewhat crisply. 'Is that where you got the bay horse?' Before he could answer, she also said, 'And the buckskin? I didn't know Mrs Morgan kept cold-blooded horses.'

The stocky man, who was also greying, put out a hand. 'You was in a fix, friend.' When Carter released his hand, he also said, 'Them boys wanted you pretty bad.'

The older woman interrupted. 'I've got dinner on the stove.'

Agnes tugged Carter's sleeve lightly

and the four of them went toward the house. As the older man held the door for his women and Carter to enter first, he grinned at Carter. 'They was goin' to hang you.'

Carter entered and removed his hat. 'For horse-stealin'?'

'That's what they had in mind. one of 'em a federal US marshal.'

'He wanted to lynch me, too?'

'No, not him, but I can understand the others. You was ridin' the Morgans' race horse. Anybody around knows that horse. He's made Emily Morgan a right good livin'.'

The older woman pointed. 'Set . . . Aggie, help me.'

After the men sat and the women were gone, the man said, 'I can't say I'd shed tears over Emily losin' her runnin' horse. She's been nothin' but trouble since her husband died. He was a nice fellow. Emily's a — '

The voice came from the kitchen. 'Adam! Not another word against Miz Morgan!'

The meal was as good, bountiful and hot as Carter expected it to be and because he was hungry he did little to keep the conversation going. He answered questions, reddened a little when he saw how the women were regarding him and, when he was finished, Adam Courtright invited him out to the front porch for a smoke. Carter did not know it at the time but Maude Courtright did not allow smoking in the house.

Aggie brought a bowl of hot water from the kitchen for her mother to wash Carter's injury. It didn't amount to much but Carter was an easy bleeder.

The conversation was lengthy and while Carter was drawn into it going back to his initial appearance in the Tumbleweed country and back even further he had no idea right at this moment how good an interrogator Aggie's mother was until the day waned along toward sundown and beyond.

By milking time, when the girl left

the house with a bucket, her father left his wife at her meticulous job with the wounded man to do other chores and the day was fast fading.

Dusk settled, the girl returned with a half-full bucket and her father paused on the porch to brush his trouser legs free of clinging weeds. It was almost time to eat again.

Maude's husband got two cups of hot coffee, sat down and was interested in what Carter could tell him about his most recent travels, and the Morgan outfit. Clearly, there was no love lost between the Courtrights and Emily Morgan. Carter put the bits and pieces together from Courtright to determine that as neighbours what didn't exactly amount to a feud came close to being one. Eventually, even Adam's woman, who was not ordinarily a person of strong aversions, added her two bits' worth.

By the time Agnes and her parents had supported each other in denigrations, Carter was convinced he had misjudged Emily Morgan: she wasn't what he'd originally thought.

Supper was a reproduction of dinner. When it was finished, Carter took an all-over bath at the miserly creek that ran west of the house a short distance, bedded down in the loft and slept like a dog until shortly before dawn when sounding coyotes passed through in a foraging pack.

When the girl called him to breakfast, the sun was showing and Adam was making a racket in the barn where four hungry horses were impatiently stamping.

They went to the house together, barely made it before some distance southward a man with the voice of a bullfrog hailed the house demanding that Carter come out onto the porch. He bellowed from the direction of the ruts that served as a road that branched off the coach road.

Adam Courtright raised an out-flung arm to prevent Carter from walking into plain sight and called back, 'Who'n hell are you, an' what d'you want?'

The reply came from a different voice south of where the original call had come from.

'We're lookin' for a feller ridin' a stole bay runnin' horse. We liked to have got him yestiddy, but a band of cattle scattered us. When we was able to continue the chase, we saw sign where him an' another feller turned off an' come up in here. His name's Carter. He's a horse-thief. Tall feller, ridin' one an' trailin' one. A bay an' a buckskin.'

Courtright answered without hesitation. 'Hasn't been no feller come in here with no two horses.'

'Mister, mind if we look around?'

'Yes, I mind. There's only me, my wife an' my daughter. If he turned up in here he more'n likely saw the buildings an' left that road goin' northerly.'

That ended the yelling back and forth, but the sound of riders fanning out north and south was distinctly audible.

Courtright spoke to his uninvited

guest in a low voice. 'Into the loft with you.'

Carter did not move. He saw horsemen ride off into the rocks and underbrush on both sides of the ruts leading into the yard. Someone told them to scatter, shoot on sight and to never mind taking Carter alive.

Adam shifted his bucket of fresh-found eggs to one hand, growled at Carter to scramble up the wall rungs, get into the loft and open the rear loft door, jump down and make a beeline for the house. Then, he walked out into the yard looking easterly, the direction from which that pursuer had called from, and yelled a warning, 'You shoot into the house where my wife'n daughter are an' you'll wish you hadn't.'

No one shot into the house, nor from it. The only movement was Courtright carrying his bucket of eggs walking toward the porch, a distance of about sixty or seventy feet.

The silence was deafening until

Courtright reached the porch and stamped his feet. The door swung inward and was slammed closed and the quiet remained unbroken outside until Courtright turned, fired in the direction of the private road and got back a fusillade until someone out there called profanely for his companions to stop shooting.

The silence returned.

9

Forted Up

Adam Courtright made a prophetic remark while levering a massive oak table into position to block bullets likely to come through a north-wall window. 'I told you, Maude.'

Her answer was waspish instead of fearful. 'You said Indians!' The basis for an argument was shattered by gunfire. In time, the men in the yard managed to reach places of advantage. Eventually, Maude broke an interval of silence by telling her husband she knew he would enjoy being attacked.

Instead of an answer from her husband one came from his daughter.

'Over a horse? Pa, we're warrin' over a stolen horse?'

Adam did not answer. He was crouching behind his barricade of furniture waiting for a target. Carter was nearby and while visibility was not as good as it might have been, it was good enough to sight movement if there was any.

Carter called out, 'Tormey? Can you hear me, Marshal Tormey?'

He got no retort until someone called back in that familiar gravelly voice from the wagon shed which was between the shop and a water-well shack. 'Carter, you damned fool, you're out-numbered an' out-gunned. Just come out on the porch where we can see you. We'll take the runnin' horse an' leave . . . You hear me, Carter?'

Agnes looked at her father. When it looked as if he was ignoring the person who called, she called back an answer. 'He hears you an' he's not comin' out. You got to come get him.'

Adam Courtright looked around at his daughter. 'Don't you say another blessed word. You hear me?'

Agnes had no opportunity to reply, gunshots peppered the house from different positions. Carter heard something fall westerly of where he was protected by an old-fashioned high-boy cupboard of oak, which was not only heavy but solid. Something inside the high-boy was smashed. It sounded like glass but it wasn't. Maude's mother had given her a New England roasting bowl. A bullet had penetrated the oak doors and smashed an elegant soup tureen.

That brought a fierce howl from Maude Courtright in the kitchen. She had fired with a double-barrelled shotgun which was kept behind the kitchen door. A man bawled from the loft sliding window of the bunkhouse Adam had not quite finished, and a kitchen shelf lost all its heirlooms, most of which broke when they hit the floor.

Maude called out, using words her daughter had never heard her use and laced as much of the barn as she could see. Agnes was more than shocked listening to Maude's profanity.

Whether Maude aimed or not, whoever had been out yonder in the barn had his own vocabulary and used it, calling Maude everything he could think of, until Adam took his wife's part in this duel and whoever had got into the loft had had enough and howled like a gutshot elk as he went down out of the loft and ran for all he was worth going northward, clear of the barn in the direction of the blacksmithing shed.

He was exposed twice; once where he passed the girl's firing position, and again when he passed Adam's place.

Both of them fired at the racing man. A few feet short of the shoeing shed, Adam Courtright's shot brought him down. Not fatally. He managed to get up onto all fours and scramble into the smithy. Agnes emptied the slide of her rifle where she had last seen the man, heard horseshoes draped from a peg go in all directions and, hurt or not, the target did not return her fire.

Maude, in her kitchen, had a sighting and yelled to her daughter she hadn't missed. She yelled that the man in the shoeing shed was squirming and rolling in the dirt near the anvil hugging one leg.

Carter got nearer the door leading out to the porch. He was uncomfortable, each time he moved he felt a sensation he had never felt before.

The girl watched him. When he began easing in the direction of the porch door, she went after him, exposing herself until they met and she grabbed his arm. He was almost upset, pushed out a hand to brace against the wall as she said, 'Lie down . . . on the floor!'

He resisted her efforts to put him down. Adam looked around. He smiled at them and gestured for Carter to do as his daughter said.

Carter got against the wall and braced himself there. Agnes stopped trying to down him.

Someone yelled from the yard. 'Adam! Can you hear me, Adam!'

Courtright's reply was brusque. 'I can hear you, Everett.'

Another voice answered, 'What do

you want? You had enough? All's we got to do is set down an' wait for night, then burn you out.'

Courtright ignored the voice and again addressed Everett. 'Ev, you'n me have tangled enough times for me to talk honest-like. I told you before . . . that woman'll use you. She'll get you killed. You want some advice? Quit her. If you want a job I'll give you one. Ev, you damned fool, loyalty is one thing . . . stayin' on to help her after her husband died is somethin' else. Ev, you got to know what she's like by now. Get on your horse, ride back an' tell her you quit an' don't even look back . . . Unless you want to hire on with me . . . Ev?'

A voice Carter recognized came from the direction of the road. 'Carter, your friend, the federal lawman left us some time ago. Whatever he's up to won't make no difference. Before he can get back you'n them folks in the house will be cooked to cinders. It's up to you.'

Adam Courtright turned toward

Carter. 'Friend of yours?'

Carter shook his head. 'He was with the deputy lawman. No friend of mine.'

Someone using a carbine shot the door. The bullet hit the latch which broke and the door flew open nearly striking the girl. It was evidently a planned tactic because a flurry of gunshots made a deafening racket and bullets came through the opening. One slug tore a framed picture off the west wall. Another slug came on an angle, narrowly missed Maude Courtright and buried itself in wall siding.

Carter fired back as did the rancher using the oak table as a shield.

Silence settled. Adam called, got no reply and looked around at Carter.

'Savin' shells,' he said, and told his daughter to go into the kitchen with her mother.

She had a Winchester rifle, not a carbine, a rifle with twice the range of a saddle gun. She shook her head and remained near Carter. She said, 'I could sneak out an' go for Harry Tompkins.'

Her father snorted in disgust. 'You couldn't get to the barn. I don't know how many's out there but you'd never make it, an' besides, you heard Harry say last week he was goin' up north an' get some teeth pulled.'

Agnes did not give up. 'Jack an' Graham'll be home.'

Courtright snorted again. 'Kids, Aggie. Hardly big enough to hold a gun let alone use one.'

The same rough-voiced individual in the vicinity of the rutted road leading to the yard tried again. 'Carter, it's not worth gettin' killed over. All we want is the horse. You just set down'n rest. We'll go to the barn an' lead him out.'

Carter called back, 'An' you got the guts to call me a horse-thief!'

The retort came curtly. 'I got a bill of sale for him.'

'You're lyin'!'

'You'll see about that. We sent back for that woman to come up here.'

Adam faced around again. 'Is he likely tellin' the truth?'

Carter shook his head. 'Ask Ev if she'd give anyone a bill of sale.'

After a long pause, Everett, the old rangeman called to Carter. 'It's the gospel truth, Bob. But even if it wasn't, no damned horse that's ever been foaled is worth gettin' shot over. Let one of 'em go to the barn.'

Carter's answer had nothing to do with the big running horse. 'Ev, what's wrong with you? You worked for them folks a long time. You told me that yourself.'

Ev called back sharply 'For him, not for her. I told her some time back I'd be leavin', couldn't stand no more of her underhanded ways. Bob, let 'em have the horse!'

From the kitchen someone fired off a scattergun. Moments later a man howled for all he was worth, broke into a wildly flinging run and dove head first into a seemingly impenetrable thicket.

In the house, Adam called a congratulation to his daughter. She answered waspishly. 'It wasn't me, it was Ma!'

For a long time there was not a sound until Carter broke the stillness. 'You fellers with Tormey, mount up an' go back where you come from.'

He got a gravelly answer. 'Them others did. Me, I'm goin' to get paid not to. Carter, for Chris'sake use your head. It'll be dark directly. You'll get burnt out . . . you'n them folks over there with you.'

From back on the road westerly someone fired off a round. Silence settled again.

Maude Courtright obeyed a womanly instinct. She made a plateful of sandwiches and sent her daughter to hand them around. Carter hadn't been conscious of hunger until the girl offered the food, then he took two of the sandwiches, holstered his six-gun and ate like a starving man. For some reason, he had a mental flashback to his initial meeting with the she-bear with whom he had shared food another time.

Shadows formed slowly. After a while

Adam said, 'Carter, most likely they pulled out.'

Carter did not think so. 'They're waitin' for full dark. Why'n hell would those men risk their necks over a horse?'

Adam's reply was quietly given. 'Pardner, you don't know the district. That runnin' horse kept them folks in groceries. Far as I know he'd never been beat but once or twice. I wouldn't risk my life to get hold of him, but I don't figure things like Emily does.'

'She's got cattle,' Carter explained.

'Danged few left. She sells 'em a few at a time; an' somethin' else, she rustles my strays that drift over on to her land but that won't last much longer. Pardner, the runnin' horse is all she's got left.'

Carter was quiet for as long as he had anything to eat and because he was not by nature an argumentative individual he did not prolong their conversation after the last crust was gone.

Maude worked in her kitchen. She

181

was hindered when her husband called to her, not to light a lamp, but after so many years she knew every nook and cranny. Occasionally, she rattled pans and her cook stove made crackling sounds. Smoke rose from the stove pipe too, but with dusk thickening it was doubtful that the besiegers could see smoke rising. But they could smell it and because hunger was not confined to the men outside, when the man with the gravelly voice trumpeted again Carter was not surprised.

'Hey, you, squatter in the house . . . you want to talk?'

Adam answered shortly, 'Nothin' to talk about. You're forcin' trouble. You're trespassin', an' as far as I'm concerned you come here for trouble an' by Gawd we're goin' to give you a bellyful.'

The man called back in the same almost friendly voice. 'Listen, mister, this ain't your trouble. All we want is that damned runnin' horse an' the feller who stole him . . . an' we'll pay you right well for a meal. That's all. We aren't goin' to try smokin' you out; just let us have the damned horse an' get your woman to feed us an' we'll pay you in greenbacks, take the horse an' leave. No more fightin'. How's that sound?'

Maude surprised her man, her daughter and Carter when she answered from the kitchen. 'Come out where I can see you, you son of a bitch, you'll get an answer . . . a twelve-gauge answer!'

Adam and his daughter were silent. Neither of them had ever heard Maude use that epithet before.

Carter stepped to one side of the open doorway, peered out and fired off two rounds, stepped back and squeezed off a third trigger pull and nothing happened.

Agnes made a circuitous rush from the kitchen, handed Carter what remained of a box of handgun loads and darted back.

Carter reloaded and waited. No answering shot came back. He pushed his way past furniture to kneel beside Adam and say, 'When it's a tad darker I'm goin' to try for the barn.'

The older man answered crisply. 'Like hell you are. They've had plenty of time to get over there themselves.'

Carter seemed not to hear Courtright as he edged toward the nearest edge of the table. It had been hit several times. Among the holes there were some that had penetrated the oak.

Adam shifted position. He had been crouching behind the table since the fight began. Carter gestured him away as Adam sprang into a low crouch with one hand outstretched. He missed when Carter came upright, sprinting toward the mud-wattle fireplace where red embers showed.

The nearest door was on his left. There was a second door in the opposite wall. It was closed. Carter went through the left-hand door and emerged in the kitchen. He paused long enough to make sure his six-gun was fully loaded before leaving the kitchen, crossing to the other door and hastening through it into a bedroom that had a window in the west wall. He hoped very hard the window would not squeak when he opened it and for one of the very rare times in his life his prayer was answered. The window not only did not make noise when he opened it, there was no screen to be wrestled with. Screens over windows were a rarity in back country ranch houses.

His side of the house had only chilly gathering darkness as he eased out until his feet touched earth.

He dropped flat down pistol up and ready. If there was anyone on the west side of the house Carter neither heard nor saw them and they didn't see him.

With a pounding heart, he got slowly upright to wait for movement or a sound.

The darkness was still forming. Carter remained against the house at his back as he worked his way toward the juncture of two walls, the westerly wall and the front one.

He stopped near that juncture, breathed deeply, crouched to peer ahead, saw no movement, gauged the distance to the barn and ran. Even in darkness movement was visible.

Someone fired. The report was loud enough for the weapon to have been a shotgun. Carter did not try to place the shooter, but if Carter had been seen he at least hadn't been hit.

He did not fire back not even when he reached the far corner of the barn.

He flattened again to listen. There was a slight rattling in the barn. It could have been a rat, a horse or a man. He edged backward to the rear passageway, hesitated, took down more deep inhalations and jerked sideways until he was in the rear opening. He crouched, expecting gunfire.

There was none. He looked over his shoulder. Nothing moved nor spoke.

Carter groped for a stall door, found one and continued to move, easterly this time until he heard an animal shifting position in one of the stalls.

He crouched at the lower half of a stall door and was working his way upright when the stalled animal stopped moving and Carter felt warm breath.

He stopped moving, raised his left hand, felt something soft and warm, came up to his full height and had the warm breath in his face on the right side.

He stopped moving, groped with the left hand, felt mane hair and beneath it warm, satiny, neck hair and, unexpectedly, a hot, wet tongue.

Few horses licked people: that was a dog's trick.

Carter groped, felt along the neck toward the withers, got licked in the face and whispered, 'You big son of a bitch!'

The horse snorted and pulled back. Carter had only a glimpse of the man before a fist as hard as stone caught him high on the same side and his knees turned watery. He swung, missed and grabbed the edge of the stall door before he collapsed.

He would have fallen except for the grip he had on the edge of the door. He reacted instinctively by twisting away and swinging his balled fist a second time. This time, too, he missed, but as his legs recovered slightly, his third blow found someone's flannel shirting material and the man he could only see as a shadow, coughed.

Carter's grip on the stall door loosened. He struggled to control his legs, felt the next strike graze his ear and tried one more time.

The man went down at his feet, not hurt nor unconscious but determined. Carter's legs stiffened. He swung both fists, felt a connection and followed his assailant to the ground.

His attacker coughed three times, wheezed and struggled to disengage from the powerful grip that held him to the ground.

Carter leaned off, aimed and fired a gnarled fist.

His attacker, who had not only been able to make it into the barn but had also detected the scraping sound of feet out back, weakened further under Carter's pummelling rock-hard fists. Carter made his last blow count before falling across the man beneath him.

His body was losing strength, but his mind warned him in his semi-conscious condition that he had to recover, and he did. He pushed himself off his unconscious adversary, sat up, breathed deeply until he could make himself arise.

He stood looking down. Whoever his attacker was he was strong enough to slowly force himself to use both hands to scrabble in the earth below and push.

He had to duplicate this effort several times before he could hold himself in an unsteady, wobbly position. He probably would have collapsed the last time except for Carter's reach which steadied the man. They looked at each other until the attacker spoke.

'You hit hard, you son of a bitch. I know you; I saw you in town with that Morgan lady.'

Carter had to strain to get the man onto his feet. He felt for the man's six-gun. The holster was empty. The gun had fallen from its leather. Carter gave the man a hard push. When he fell Carter stepped past and retrieved the man's Colt, growled for him to get up and cocked the gun by way of emphasis.

This time he didn't have to help the attacker. He stood up, wiped his face on a faded sleeve and kept his eyes on the cocked pistol as he said, 'Mister, this ain't my fight. I was deputized to ride with the law. Are you Carter?'

Strength returned slowly, but it returned. Carter nodded his head. 'I'm Carter; who're you?'

'Les Bledsoe. I got the harness works in Tumbleweed.'

Carter considered his prisoner. On one side, stalled horses had their heads over the bottom door. Carter eased the

190

hammer down on the gun in his hand. 'You know those folks in the house?'

His unsteady captive answered shortly, 'The Courtrights? I know 'em, but I had no idea you was friends to them.'

Carter recognized the big bay horse looking out at him. He said, 'We're goin' to the house. You see that bay horse watchin' us?'

'Yes. What of it?'

'I'll be leavin' on him after I take you over yonder.'

'Carter, you could just let me go.'

Carter showed a mocking slight smile. 'Yeah, I could. I could also blow your damned head off.'

The battered, rumpled and soiled attacker said, 'I got a better idea. You'n me saddle up an' get the hell away from here, an' when we're far enough you go one way'n I'll go another way.'

Carter did not lose his bitter, small smile. 'Walk out the back door, and stop. I'll be behind you with your gun. *Walk*!'

Bledsoe walked. Where he turned left beyond the door he stopped. There was more darkness in the night and it was colder than it had been.

Carter herded the man to the furthest corner, told him to get down on all fours and head for the yonder porch. Bledsoe obeyed without looking over his shoulder which might have encouraged him to run for it. Carter was also down on all fours with Bledsoe's six-gun in his holster.

10

Bargainers

It had been quiet too long. Carter crawled, listening for sound of which there was none. Bledsoe started to say something and Carter cursed him into silence.

When they reached the porch and Bledsoe climbed the steps he leaned to arise. Carter put his foot on the man's back. 'Stay down!'

Carter moved past, rattled the door and when Maude opened it one-handed with her scattergun in the other hand, Carter said, 'Get up!'

Maude was too surprised to speak as both men walked past her into the dark parlour where Adam and his daughter stood like statues.

Carter used his fisted six-gun to prod his captive almost as far as Adam's upended oaken table, as he said curtly, 'Caught this one in the barn.'

Adam leaned aside his carbine, stood up and brusquely nodded his head. 'I know him. He's got the harness works in town.' Adam poked Bledsoe in the chest with a rigid finger. 'You're helpin' those bastards?'

Bledsoe's reply was a whine. 'Mister Courtright, gettin' deputized is worth four bits a day, it ain't nothin' personal.'

Adam's family and Carter were like statues, silent and standing still. Bledsoe was encouraged and spoke again. 'They deputized two of us. Me'n Tom Leary.'

Maude spoke abruptly. 'You'n the storekeeper?'

'Yes, ma'am. Sheriff Cassidy was gone an' no one else wanted to join.' Bledsoe had a little to add. 'Deputy Hanlon said there'd be a bounty on Carter.'

Adam scowled. 'For what?'

'Horse-stealin'. He said Mrs Morgan told him she'd pay to get her runnin' horse back an' to see this feller hanged.'

Carter went to a rickety chair and sat down. He told Bledsoe he was lying and the captive vigorously shook his head.

Adam did not take his eyes off the posseman when he told his daughter to get a lass rope off its nail on the back porch.

The moment she was gone, Adam also told Bledsoe to sit flat down on the floor and at the look he got from the captive he also said, 'Well, it's better'n me shootin' you. Set down!'

Maude took the shotgun with her when she went out of sight in the kitchen. When her daughter returned with the coiled rope, Maude came from the kitchen with a thick sandwich in one hand which she handed to Carter.

Neither of them said a word as they watched Maude's husband and daughter pass the rope back and forth as they tied Bledsoe starting at the ankles and working their way up. His arms were lashed behind his back. Until they finished and got clear, Bledsoe did not make a sound, but afterwards, while straining to see how well he was bound, he addressed Bob Carter.

'This ain't goin' to do you any good. When that lady gets here, her and Deputy Hanlon'll confirm every blessed word I said.'

No one answered. With time passing, the tied prisoner was ignored as though he wasn't on the parlour floor.

Carter finished the sandwich Maude had made for him and cracked the door a few inches to listen. He heard a shod horse turn in onto the Courtright's roadway, closed the door, leaned against it and said, 'Won't be long now. A rider just came in. It'll be Mrs Morgan.'

The next time he peered out, he noticed the approach of another visitor; dawn was coming. He closed the door, ignored the others and sat down tiredly.

The quiet was broken by the voice of the deputy sheriff. 'Mr Courtright, Mrs Morgan's here. She wrote me out a warrant for Carter. He's lucky it didn't happen in town. He'd have been hanged. She'll forget about you folks aidin' a horse-thief, all you got to do is push him out of the house. Courtright, you hear me?'

Adam leaned aside his carbine, stood up behind his oaken bulwark and answered, 'Come an' get him, Deputy. You trespassin' on my deeded land is bad enough, but workin' up some drumhead warrant ain't good enough. Take Mrs Morgan an' them fellers with you and get the hell back where you come from. Mrs Morgan, you hear me? Carter didn't steal your horse. You owe him that much for workin' for you.'

Carter shook his head. He hadn't worked for her long enough to have earned a horse. Any horse.

He went over where Adam Courtright was leaning and called out, 'Ma'am, put a price on your horse.'

He got back a reply that didn't surprise him. 'Bob, you'll never have enough money to pay for my horse. He's just plain not for sale.'

The deputy was pleased and it reflected in his voice. 'Carter! He isn't for sale. You took him out of her barn without permission. Mister, that's horse-stealin' accordin' to the law. He isn't for sale an' you took him anyway. I'll get him back for her. That's my job.'

Adam Courtright nudged Carter. 'Leave it be. They don't want to settle, they want to fight . . . I know somethin' about that.'

Courtright took his stand, aimed and fired. Someone yelped. Ninety-nine out of a hundred 'sound shots' never connect, but this one had come close enough to startle someone.

The woman tried again. 'Bob? This is Emily. Let me talk to you.'

Adam leaned aside the carbine again, looked at Carter and shrugged. 'Talk to her if you want to.'

Carter hung fire; for a fact she was a right presentable female woman, he'd thought that the first time he'd seen her. Agnes came close, looked steadily at Carter and said softly, 'Talk to her

. . . let her have the horse.'

Instinctively, he held out a hand. She took it. Colour mounted in her face. He squeezed. She squeezed back. He released her hand and nodded. He would talk to Emily Morgan.

Maude was the worrier. When the arrangements had been made she told her husband they would shoot Carter the moment he left the house. She wanted Adam to prevent the meeting. He consoled her. Agnes, too, but she stood silent and motionless when Carter went to the door; only after he had closed the door after himself did she walk stiffly to the kitchen door and into her mother's arms.

A flight of noisy crows passed above the house. Their raucous noise faded as they went northward. Adam shook his head. His neighbour had just sewn a field in wheat.

He was jerked back to reality when Emily Morgan called a warm greeting to Carter as they came close out in the centre of the yard.

Emily exuded pleasantness and for a fact she was an attractive woman. She offered her hand. He looked past, saw a man half hidden by tree shade and said, 'Emily . . .'

Her response was quick. 'Bob, it's not entirely the horse, I'm fond of him too . . . ' She let the words trail off.

'Emily, I don't know how to explain it but there are times when animals . . . '

'Bob, he's just a horse.'

'Maybe. I'm not sure you'll understand, but maybe it's just that being a loner, I . . . Brown Billy is more than just a running horse to me.'

'Can I ask you a question, Bob?'

'Yes. Fire away.'

'Did you ever think of having a family?'

'I think I told you, Emily, I have a son. He's young and — '

'Your wife, Bob?'

'She died some years back. I've been on the move ever since.'

'Bob?'

'Yes'm?'

'Would you settle down? The bay horse would be a wedding present.'

He was shocked speechless. He cleared his throat, shot a quick look over his shoulder and shifted his stance. 'You could do better, Emily,' he said, and wondered if the lines in her face matched whatever it was that made it difficult for him to like her.

'I need a husband, Bob. Running the ranch by myself . . . I'm going deeper in the hole every year.'

'You have Everett. He's savvy about cattle an' all.'

'Bob, Ev's old enough to be my father.'

He started to correct that, caught himself in time and grinned at her.

She blushed, smiled, and suddenly they both laughed. He raised his hat, scratched and lowered the hat into place. She said, 'Bob . . . ?'

He was reaching for some way to say it without hurting her feelings. 'Emily, could we be neighbours?'

Emily's expression underwent a swift change. 'Neighbours?' The change in her was so abrupt and forceful he was having trouble believing it.

She still had colour in her face. The only thing that changed was her expression. 'I'll take the horse and go home. If I owe you anything for the day or two you worked for me, ride home with me and I'll pay you.'

'You don't owe me anything. The horse, Emily: put a price on him.'

There was a noticeable edge to her voice when she answered him. 'I told you, Bob, you can have him. We could . . . you could ride him over to Tumbleweed with me. The preacher's name is Fred Dallin.'

The crows returned flying faster and with less squawking. In the house Adam Courtright watched them and said softly, 'Shy one bird, Maude. I'd say the neighbours is back. The crows got to find another grain field.'

As the birds and their noise retreated southward, Carter let go a long, quiet sigh. 'Emily . . . ?'

Her retort was given in one word and it had the same sharp edge to it. 'What!'

'Another time, maybe. Another place.'

'I'll get the horse, Bob.'

'No, ma'am. He stays right where he is. I'll fight you to the last bullet. Sell him to me, Emily, before someone gets hurt.'

She was stiff with indignation. He had seen mood changes in people many times, but never so abruptly nor so swiftly. 'I wouldn't sell him to you if you were the last man on earth!'

She started to move, to pass him on his far side in the direction of the barn. He instinctively moved to block her. They were almost face to face so he did not have to raise his voice when he said 'The horse stays here.' He had more to say, but didn't get the chance to say it. She raised a hand to clear him out of her way and he caught her by the wrist.

Somewhere behind her a fair distance, a man moved from the shade of a tree. Carter flung her aside as the man went for his hip holster. Carter was fast. The shots sounded simultaneously. Carter was wrenched sideways, the man near the tree went down backwards under impact and did not move.

Maude screamed from the house as Adam fired from behind his oaken fortification.

Someone fired from the vicinity of the shoeing shed, missed Carter completely. The bullet slammed into the front logs of the house.

Carter ran instinctively but desperately. Where that shot had torn his sleeve his arm felt warmly moist.

Adam got off a round in the direction of the smithy and Maude's scattergun had a kick-back that almost took her down backwards.

Agnes had the door open. Carter went past her into the parlour before stopping. Agnes slammed and barred the door. A bullet that seemed to come from nowhere smashed into the door.

Adam yelled something that Carter

did not understand. Adam used his long-gun barrel as a pointer and yelled something that incoming gunfire made it impossible to distinguish. Adam made a whirling gesture with one arm and yelled again. This time the incoming round clipped the edge of his oaken table and he dropped, not hit, but momentarily startled out of his wits.

Carter thought Adam had been hit and bounded across to where Adam was floundering. He grabbed the old man's arm to pull him out of harm's way with Adam squealing like a shoat caught in a gate and trying to gesture with his rifle.

Maude came, squealing and groaning. She dropped beside her husband on the left side. Their daughter went to her knees on the opposite side.

Adam struggled to use the rifle as a pointer. There was too much commotion, so he relinquished his grip on the rifle, lashed out to free himself, and yelled, 'Emily! Someone downed Emily!'

Maude was not deterred, but her daughter jumped up, crossed to the oak table bulwark and crouched where she could see the yard and beyond. She did not make a sound but held one hand to her face.

The wild flurry of shooting ended. That depth of silence returned and lasted until a voice Carter recognized, hailed the house.

'Carter? You all right, Carter?'

Carter knew that voice. Tormey must have returned from Tumbleweed, if he actually ever went there. Carter called back, 'Good enough. Is that you, Tormey?'

'It's me. Is it safe for me to come over there?'

Adam Courtright answered. 'Come ahead. Mind them bastards out there with you.'

Tormey delayed his reply long enough to make sure his companions heard the exchange and would not fire their weapons.

Adam was being brushed off by his

206

wife after he got back upright. His daughter pulled a long oak splinter from his shirt and handed it to her mother as she said, 'Keepsake.'

Maude accepted the sliver without smiling or speaking.

Carter drank a large glass of water before leaving the house. At the door, Agnes brushed him with one hand. When he faced around she leaned and kissed him hard.

Her mother and father were no more surprised than Carter was. He seemed to freeze for several seconds before raising both hands to pull her close when he returned the kiss. Her smile was quavery when she spoke too softly for her parents to hear.

'Don't turn your back on 'em Mr Carter.'

He leaned, kissed her squarely on the mouth, and said, 'Cover my back, ma'am.'

'Agnes, not ma'am,' she corrected him, and closed the door after him and leaned on it with both her parents staring at her.

Two men carried Emily toward the barn where the daylight scantily reached. Deputy Federal Marshal Tormey advanced more than halfway, and when Carter came up, extended his hand as he said, 'You look like the wrath of Gawd. Anyone worse off in the house?'

Carter forced a smile. 'No. We had plenty of cover in there.' Carter looked past the federal deputy in the direction of the road. 'You bring more reinforcements from town?'

Tormey nodded. 'Three. Couldn't get more, not even Sheriff Cassidy. Seems he's got no use for the Morgan woman. He had some crazy idea she give her runnin' horse to someone so's she could collect the insurance on him. Which is a damned lie. I got that old highbinder Morse an' one of his nephews locked up in the *calabozo* back in Tumbleweed. Carter? You got her runnin' horse?'

Carter jerked his head. 'In the barn. Tried to buy him off her. She'd let me have the horse . . . a trade for somethin' she had in mind.'

Carter saw several men heading for the barn in plain sight. 'Marshal, there's no love lost around here. To keep more folks from gettin' hurt it might'n be a bad idea if you'd send those lads back where they came from. What's left of this mess can be thrashed out in the house over a cup of coffee.'

Tormey shook his head. That had been the longest uninterrupted conversation he had ever heard from Bob Carter.

Tormey made a tight little lopsided smile as he was turning away. 'I'll do that,' he said, and paused to look toward the house. 'You sure those folks in the house won't shoot me?'

Carter was sure. 'They didn't have no hand in this. Those boys ridin' with the deputy sheriff brought it on. I'll wait at the house.'

Tormey watched three men come to the barn's front opening and called to them. 'Want me to send for the medicine man in Tumbleweed? If he's in town I'll come back with him.'

A man Carter did not know answered for himself and his companions. 'We stopped the bleedin'. She wants to go home. If it's all the same to you, Marshal, we'll take her home an' wait down there for you'n the doctor.'

Tormey nodded briskly and returned his attention to Carter. 'Who shot her?' he asked.

Carter had no idea beyond the simple fact that no one at the house had fired during his palaver with Emily Morgan until after she and Carter had parleyed.

Someone had shot her. How badly Carter had no idea, but, as he watched the marshal go back toward the boulder-strewn area of the Courtright turn-road, he thought he would ride over to the Morgan ranch with the men who were rigging a horse-stretcher for Emily Morgan. He had to work something out with her to get a bill of sale for Brown Billy.

Adam Courtright was waiting on the porch when Carter got back to the house. They talked, with Maude and her daughter listening where the door was open a crack. Both women heard Adam ask if Carter intended to come back. They heard him say he would return as quickly as he could, and left the three Courtrights watching as he strode toward the barn.

11

Two Graves, Two Visitors

There was nothing easy about rigging three blankets into a horse stretcher. It required two placid animals to start with and after having several animals kick and rear, squawl and bite, they got two horses that would stand for a highly odd carry-all to be rigged. One of the horses was Carter's buckskin horse. The buckskin, which had never had such a peculiar arrangement made fast to it, got along well with an elderly pelter belonging to Adam Courtright and the cavalcade left the yard.

Adam might have ridden along, but with both his women insisting that he stay home he turned back.

Maude's insistence was well-founded. Three of the posse riders had been injured during the fight. Two of them were unable to ride and the third one had a slantwise bullet gash across his hams. He could have ridden, but Maude helped him to the house where Agnes brought bedding and made a satisfactory bedroll on the parlour floor.

Two of the injured men were casually known to the Courtrights. One was the saddle and harness proprietor from Tumbleweed. He became a casualty while a prisoner on the floor, tied and face down, had rolled over broken glass for protection from gunfire and had ended up with several gashes in his haste.

The other man was the storekeeper, Tom Leary. He was the casualty who had been grazed crossways behind and below the belt. Shotgun pellets at a considerable range did not kill people, but the process of digging out each small pellet was painful. What was worse was the local storekeeper was very uncomfortable with the women tending his injury. He had known the Courtright women since they had come into the Tumbleweed country. Adamantly he told Maude she could work on him but he didn't even want Agnes in the same room.

Adam worked hard to prevent laughing. Agnes got busy in the kitchen heating water and making bandages until her mother had finished removing pellets and with a perfectly straight face created a diaper-sized bandage for the storekeeper.

Old Everett rode stirrup with Carter. They carried on a desultory conversation. The nearer the cavalcade with its litter got to the Morgan place, the dragooned riders from town drifted away. They took a shortcut to Tumbleweed. The deputy took the men he had reason to lock up. When they turned off at the road leading to the Morgan ranch, Carter interrupted his talk with old Ev to lean and stroke the big running horse's neck.

The last words between the deputy and Carter were brief. Carter reined in the direction of the Morgan wagon ruts leading to the big house and the yard. Emily had held up well until Carter and the lawman parted.

Emily was crying. Ev and Carter took care of the animals after helping carry Emily inside and upstairs to her bedroom. They saw the top buggy turn in and Ev left Carter to escort the medical man upstairs in the main house.

Carter took Brown Billy out of his stall, washed him all over from bucketed water and filled the manger after he put the running horse back in his stall.

He was washing his buckskin horse when Ev returned. He stood in the rear barn opening watching Carter at the trough briefly, then disappeared back inside the barn.

Carter was in no hurry. He eventually finished with his buckskin and took it back to be stalled and fed as he had done with Brown Billy.

Old Ev was rigging out a brown horse with sunken places over each eye.

The horse was in good shape. There was no reason for him not to be. Everett had been riding him when he had turned in at the Morgan outfit looking for work and that had been quite a number of years earlier. Ev rarely rode his own horse, but he was rigging it out now as Carter pitched feed for the buckskin.

Carter walked over. Ev ignored him until Carter said, 'You goin' to Tumbleweed?'

Ev reached for the cinch and answered while his back was to Carter. 'No . . . not Tumbleweed anyway.' He straightened up to feed the latigo through the cinch ring, still with his back to Carter.

'I'm leavin', boy. It's over. I been here a long time.'

Carter went to sit on a nearby horseshoe keg. He was still sitting there when Everett returned with a bedroll that seemed not to have been unrolled in a very long time. When he slapped it behind the cantle, dust flew.

Carter ignored the bedroll and the dust. 'Where are you goin', Ev?'

'Well, maybe as far from the Tumbleweed country as I can get. Maybe down to Laredo. I had a sister lived there. She died some time back. She left two growin' boys an' her husband Will.' Ev turned toward Carter. 'If a man's got boys as kin, he'd ought to be around where he can help them grow up . . . Mr Carter.'

Carter took the sarcasm without batting an eye. 'What about Emily, Ev?'

'What about her? I worked for her'n her man, never hid out an' loafed. She hasn't paid me since her running horse was stoled some months ago. I saw her do some things that I made excuses for her about. Bob, stay with her; this is a good ranch. Don't let her sell down any more cattle. She can worry it through until next autumn when she'll have a sizeable bunch of fat yearlings to sell.

'She don't need to put her mark on other folk's cattle. She can make it, but she's got to quit spendin' money like it grows on trees. I know, her husband spoilt hell out of her, but them days is over.'

The physician came to the barn to get his rig and the animal that pulled it.

He wasn't as old as Everett but he was older than Carter, who got off the horseshoe keg to get the horse, lead it outside and harness it.

The physician and Ev didn't exchange ten words before the doctor came out where Carter was buckling harness. He did not get in the way, but when Carter finished harnessing and ran the lines back to the seat and moved aside for the doctor to get into his rig, he leaned, patted the horse and addressed Carter.

'You know who shot her?'

Carter had been standing there when she'd been shot, but he had no idea who shot her.

'No, sir; I think whoever he was didn't mean to hit her. There was a lot of noise out there.'

'It was broad daylight,' the doctor said. 'You'll be Carter?'

'Yes, I'm Carter.'

The physician evened up the lines and hoisted himself into the buggy. It sagged as he settled, looked toward the house, looked at old Ev who was standing in the barn's wide opening, and finally his gaze returned to Carter. He put both lines in one hand, fished inside his coat and brought forth the hand holding a folded piece of paper. 'For you,' he said. 'She gave it to me to have it taken down yonder to have it registered with the assessor.'

Carter did not take the paper. He looked at it and said, 'Give it to who?'

'The assessor. The feller in our county seat, to have it made of record. Take it, Carter! You can have it recorded, you don't need me to do it. *Take* it!'

Carter took it, the medicine man nodded, started to snap the lines, seemed to change his mind and said, 'There's someone hurt over at the Courtright place?'

Carter nodded and watched the

doctor drive out the ranch road to the main road and turn south where he would end up at Adam's ranch.

Everett seemed fixed in the barn doorway when he addressed Carter. 'Well, boy, what you waitin' for, the Second Coming? What's the paper say?'

Carter walked into barn shade before unfolding the paper. He stood a long time reading and rereading it before he let the hand holding the paper hang at his side while he slowly faced the doorway where Ev was standing. Ev said, 'Time's wastin', I better finish up here an' be on my way.' Ev fidgeted. 'I expect it'd only be the decent thing to go tell Emily I'm leavin'.'

As the older man started to move, Carter stopped him. 'Hold it, Ev, never mind tellin' her anything.'

'Why? What're you talkin' about?'

'She's dead.'

'What!'

Carter walked over where Ev was standing, eyes wide. 'That medicine

220

man told me . . . she died while he was with her.'

'That can't be, Carter. She took all that jarrin' from Courtright's place.'

'Maybe, Ev. Maybe that's what finished her off. Go see for yourself. An' there's that kid; he's dead too. If you pull out that leaves me to do the buryin'.'

Everett was thinking beyond that. 'An' the ranch?'

Carter handed Ev the paper the doctor had given him. Ev was a slow reader. Very slow. He had only scarcely learned to read one winter when Emily Morgan's husband had tried to teach him. He handed the paper back with an embarrassed look. 'Read it to me,' he said, and went over to the horseshoe keg where he sat down.

Carter read the paper aloud, saw the baffled look on the older man's face and reread the paper, more slowly and louder this time.

Everett said, 'For Chris'sake . . . she barely knew you. Why would she leave everything to you?'

Carter made no attempt to unravel that mystery. It had occurred to him also.

He leaned in the doorway. 'You told me it's a good ranch.'

'It is. While her man was alive they lived good. Only after he died . . . that's why I'm leavin'. I've watched her hire rustlers for riders'n sell off stock she should've kept.'

'Ev? I've got a notion. I never in my life owned much, but I've worked a lot of outfits for others. My idea is that . . . you stay; we'll work the place together. It's nothin' you haven't been doin'. Pay'll be whatever she was payin' you until we get the outfit makin' its way, then twice the pay.'

The older man made a swipe at a blue-tailed fly and shifted his seat. He didn't say anything for a long time then he said weakly, 'I got all my gatherings on the horse. It's an old horse, but if you standin' there was her husband you'd say, 'Take it an' good luck'.'

Carter continued to lean without speaking. Eventually, Ev stood up. He still did not look at Carter, but he led his rigged-out horse further into the barn and with his back to the wide front doorway and the man leaning there, freed up the lashings behind the cantle of his saddle, led the horse out back, removed the bridle and, still with his back to Carter, watched the horse put his tail over his back and hightail it in the distant direction of other horses.

When he finally turned he went back as far as the corner where hand implements were kept, selected two shovels and a crowbar as tall as he was, walked back where Carter stood and held out one of the shovels. 'You're youngern stronger'n I am. You carry her out where I'll be diggin'. That'll be beside where her man's buried. It'll take all day havin' to bury the both of 'em.'

Carter took the shovel, nodded to the older man, left the shovel propped and struck out for the house.

He didn't look back. He passed through the kitchen; he was hungry right up until he started climbing the stairs.

He had seen his share of dead people. He had never liked it in past times and he did not like it right now.

Without looking her in the face, he rolled her over, wrapped her in the blankets and picked her up. It was awkward returning down the stairs, but he made it and outside in fresh clean air he looked for Ev, saw him and carried her where a flesh-coloured cement plaque marked her husband's grave.

Ev looked up from his digging. 'You forgot your shovel.'

Carter put down his burden and went back for the shovel. When he got back Ev was sitting in tree shade. He made a gesture. 'Help yourself. It's got to be deeper. Bob, I been thinkin'. You got a boy?'

'Yes.'

'Has he been around a workin' cattle outfit?'

'No. Not that I know.'

'How old is he?'

'I'm not plumb sure. I think he's fourteen, maybe fifteen.'

'You want to go get him, bring him back here?'

Carter was digging. He stopped and leaned on the shovel. 'Maybe. Maybe he won't want to come.'

'You go make the effort. It'd be nice to have a young'un on the place. The both of us got to learn to laugh. It's been a long time for me. Maybe for you too. What d'ya think?'

'Ev, I was on my way south to see the boy when I landed here. Ev . . . ?'

'What?'

'You got kin?'

'Yes, I got 'em.'

'That's where you was goin'?'

'Well, I sure thought on it. Couple years back I met a feller who was lookin' for me . . . a lawman from over in Arizona.' Ev stood up, drank from a water bottle he'd brought along, put the bottle in moist earth and faced Carter.

'They was lookin' for a pair of coach robbers with the same last name as mine.' Carter stepped out of the hole, Ev stepped in, plunged his shovel in moist earth, leaned on it looking straight at Carter. 'My nephews! It's too late for me to go home and maybe help raise those lads to be decent. We're gettin' down there. It's got to be somewhere betwixt four an' five feet deep.'

When Carter took his turn in the grave he paused in his digging to show a lopsided grin to his companion.

'Ev, it's not supposed to be . . . you understand?'

'That's deep enough, lend me a hand.'

They put the woman wrapped like a mummy into the grave. It was a good fit. Covering her didn't take long. Ev moved southward a yard or so and plunged his shovel into the earth.

Carter said nothing. He was conscious of the sun's position. They would do the whole thing over again before sundown.

Ev ignored time. He also ignored conversation until he said,

'You'd better go to town and take her paper with you.'

Carter drank deeply from the water bottle before agreeing and asking Ev to go with him.

The older man shrugged and assented. 'Maybe they'll need a witness. We better leave early, Bob? What was this lad's name?'

Carter didn't know and that annoyed him. He had been a Morse captive long enough to have heard the name but for the life of him he could not remember having heard. He shook his head. 'Sheriff Cassidy's got a feller in his jailhouse that'll know.'

Ev was satisfied with that. It only barely mattered; every grave was supposed to have a name to it.

By the time the water bottle was empty, they had the second grave ready for occupancy. The older man said he'd go for the lad and headed for the main house.

Carter sat in shade. Ev had taken the empty water jug with him. Carter's thirst wasn't more than a mildly nagging sensation.

He rolled and lighted a cigarette. He was sweaty, having difficulty believing what had happened to him out of a clear sky and reread the paper giving him everything, land, cattle, buildings. He did something he hadn't done since childhood, he dropped his hat in the grass, lowered his head and gave thanks for the condition that had in only a couple of days made him a comfortably well-off ranch owner from a saddle bum with nothing more than he could stand up in, and his buckskin horse.

Burying young Morse required more time. For one thing, being sufficiently discoloured that the men avoided looking at him, and it bothered them both that he had died so young. Ev tried to ease the discomfort by telling Carter the lad probably wasn't real healthy and thinking back, Carter thought the old man had favoured him over the older boy.

When they finished mounding and tamping, Ev suggested that they let it go a day or two before they made markers.

They half-emptied the water jug, went to the corral trough to wash. As Ev was drying off, he said, 'Partner, we got company.'

Carter thought the top buggy belonged to the medicine man. Ev shook his head as they walked in the direction of the barn. 'It's Arch Cassidy, I recognize the horse and the rig.'

They waited. When the rig wheeled up in front of the house, then angled in the direction the two men were standing, Ev's brow wrinkled into a deep, quizzical frown.

'That scrawny feller on the off side of Cassidy, he's Gus Featherstone, the legal light an' half-assed banker in Tumbleweed.'

Carter watched the rig halt and said what was barely audible. 'I didn't see no bank in Tumbleweed.'

'There's no sign, but he opened the bank for business last winter. They told me he's doin' right well.'

Ev called a greeting to the visitors which only the sheriff returned as he dropped a tether weight and climbed out of the rig. Arch Cassidy was average height and overweight. He tipped the scales close to 240 pounds which was one of the reasons he preferred a buggy to horseback.

Cassidy made the introductions and when that had been taken care of he nudged the scrawny man who stepped forward and cleared his throat while groping inside his suit coat for a crisply folded piece of paper, cleared his throat again and his small, pale eyes went from Ev to Carter before he said, 'I've got a deed to the Morgan holdings.' He held out the folded paper.

Neither Carter nor Ev took the paper. Carter fished in his pocket and brought forth his signed deed.

Cassidy looked out where there were three mounded graves, two of which had mounds of moist earth. He said, 'Ev, you buried her?'

Ev nodded. 'Her an' a lad who was sickly when he rode in an' died a day or so back.'

Carter addressed the scrawny individual, the only man in Tumbleweed who wore a necktie. 'Mister Featherstone, read this. It's a signed deed to everything you see and most of what you don't see.'

The scrawny man took Carter's paper in his free hand while continuing to hold his own folded paper.

He read in total silence. Sheriff Cassidy seemed uncomfortable, his gaze constantly shifting. When Featherstone handed Carter back his paper he said, 'Isn't notarized, Mr Carter. Anyone could have drawn that up an' signed it.'

Ev scuffed his feet before saying, 'That's the same as callin' a man a liar, Featherstone.'

The pale-eyed man barely looked at old Ev. He addressed Carter.

'This here is my deed. Take it. It's been notarized over in the county seat. It's as legal as they can get to be.'

Ev was ready to speak when Carter spoke first. 'Mister, that there deed of mine was signed by Mrs Morgan before she died.'

Cassidy asked what had happened and Carter told him about the fight at the Courtright place and told him to ask his deputy, who had been over there during the shoot-out.

Sheriff Cassidy replied curtly. He hadn't seen his deputy in several days but he certainly would talk to him the next time their paths crossed.

The necktie wearer showed disapproval of the conversation getting away from him and reiterated his earlier contention with some additions.

'My deed was done right. The seal's there plain as day.'

Ev's eyes narrowed. 'Did Mrs Morgan go over to the county seat with you to get your paper notarized?'

Featherstone's face got pinkish red.

'Yes; couple of days ago.'

Ev looked at Bob Carter. 'That's when you'n her rode to town, Bob. She was plenty coyote, but she was never in two places at the same time. I know; I worked for her'n her husband somethin' like eleven years.'

Featherstone handed back Carter's paper and faced the sheriff. 'I told you, Arch.'

Sheriff Cassidy was wiping sweat off his face and neck when he spoke. 'Gents, my job is to set things to right accordin' to the law.' He looked at Featherstone. 'Don't make a damn, Gus. After listenin' to you on the ride out here I figured what I'm goin' to tell both of you now. This ain't sheriffin' business; this is for fee lawyers'n maybe a judge to say what's right an' what's wrong.'

Featherstone regarded the lawman without blinking. 'Arch, you saw my paper. The place belongs to me. I want these two fellers off my ranch by tomorrow. Your job is to see to it.'

Cassidy reddened as he faced Ev and Carter. 'You heard, gents, but I got to get some legal talk before I do anythin', Featherstone. I'll need two maybe three days to see them off the ranch. Don't argue. You've been talkin' about rights; well, I got rights too an' that includes bein' plumb positive that whatever I do is what the law says I got to do. You want to ride back with me? Let's go.'

Sheriff Cassidy allowed no time for Featherstone to speak. He walked all the way to his rig, hoisted the tether weight, put it in the box behind the seat and turned.

His companion went to the far side and climbed in. He looked straight ahead as Cassidy came close to tipping the rig as he grunted and groaned up in beside the smaller man, threw a wave backwards without looking around and talked up his horse.

Carter and Ev remained fixed in place by the barn watching the buggy curl dust all the way to the main road, turn left and go toward town in a loose trot.

Ev said, 'That miserable, little, scrawny son of a bitch. I've heard how that bastard does business ever since he's been in the country. Carter, I'd be right proud to ride along with you. She didn't sign no paper of his an' that miserable little scruff's never been out here to my knowledge. Emily's husband wouldn't have allowed him on the ranch. Carter, Doc didn't know the paper had to be officially signed — what he called notarized — you don't suppose we could write something on it?'

Carter shook his head. 'I'll go to town and see if the doctor'd go over with us an' take an oath she signed the paper, gave it to him an' told him to follow her instructions before she died.'

Ev had an objection. 'Boy, I've known Doc since he come out here. Might be better if I went an' talked to him.'

Carter hesitated a long moment

before nodding reluctantly. Dusk was edging closer by the minute when Ev left the yard. Carter watched him. He had given the paper Emily had signed to him and Ev, whose habit was to favour anything he was riding, did so now. Instead of riding hell for leather, he put his mount into an easy lope and held him to it the full distance to Tumbleweed.

12

The Road Back

The doctor had been called out to deliver a baby. Ev reddened. It would be dark before long. The doctor's wife was accustomed to impatient visitors. She assured Ev the doctor would be along shortly. He had delivered dozens of babies and this time he had been called out a half-hour ago.

She took Ev into her parlour, made him a cup of tea and left him sitting on the edge of an ornate sofa to drink tea and fidget.

The woman returned. She knew Emily Morgan was dead and she was imbued with her share of female curiosity.

She asked questions which Ev answered with no enthusiasm. He had no idea who had shot Emily Morgan, which was a great disappointment to the woman; otherwise, there wasn't much Ev could say that her husband hadn't already told her.

When the doctor returned, he avoided the parlour long enough to have a two-swallow visit with bottled Johnny Walker.

The woman left the parlour when Ev stood up to shake the doctor's hand and, being a direct individual, explained why he had come.

The baby's delivery had been difficult and tiring. Johnny Walker helped but not for long.

Ev repeated the reason for his visit twice before the doctor agreed to go with Ev.

His unknowing wife brought them both a small glass from the kitchen. The doctor downed his in a leisurely manner. Ev dropped his straight down and permitted only a scant moment or two to pass before urging the medicine man's co-operation. All that was required was the doctor's oath that he had written the last testament of the Morgan woman, and witnessed Emily Morgan's signing of the paper. After Johnny Walker's third jolt, the doctor told Ev he would meet Ev and Carter at the Morgan place about sun-up and accompany them to the county seat as their witness.

The doctor had had a trying day since dawn. Ev, too, had put in an arduous twelve or more hours. He wanted Ev to linger, have another couple of swallows of popskull and Ev sat through one more drink then headed home.

Carter was waiting with a light glowing in the parlour of the main house. He was sitting in a rocker on the porch that faced the roadway and he, too, primed Everett with an interesting result. Ev cared for his animal first then went over to the porch, sat down and fell asleep in another rocker on the porch of the main house.

Carter held a rambling one-sided conversation about several different topics which included how Emily Morgan had cozened Ev into roping, tying and marking a big Courtright bull calf.

It became one of those confidences that old Ev carried to the grave with him. Everett not only carried it to his grave with him but so did the man sitting beside him on a moonless night on the Morgan ranch's front porch.

The following morning, they left when the medicine man showed up. It was a fairly lengthy ride to the county seat and Johnny Barleycorn not only rode with them, he also was waiting at the county courthouse. The county registrar's daughter had been married the previous evening, which accounted for the county clerk's adequate but haphazard compliance with his chore of recording the testament Carter presented to him to be made of record.

On the ride back, there was an interruption no one anticipated.

Mid-way, they met a pair of riders heading for the county seat. One of them was Arch Cassidy's deputy, Rory Hanlon. His companion was the same scrawny, pale-eyed man named Featherstone who had been in the barnyard yesterday to press his claim to ownership of the Morgan ranch.

The deputy was friendly and willing to sit awhile and visit. Carter was also willing, but Ev wasn't. Ev was a learned stockman with no acting ability at all. After greetings had been exchanged, old Ev blurted out a statement that held the others silent. He said, 'Miss Emily's hand-wrote paper she gave to the medicine man was recorded no more'n an hour ago. Mr Featherstone, go see for yourself.' The deputy's smile died aborning. He looked at the man on his off side. 'You heard that, Mr Featherstone?'

The only man in the group who was wearing a necktie acted as though he hadn't heard. He looked steadily and unwaveringly at Carter. 'You figure you'd get over here early an' cut me out with some under-the-table fixings

. . . mister, it won't work. I've got a legal claim.'

Ev answered that statement, too. 'Go ahead an' try it. Carter's paper is already done legal. Your trouble is you don't get up early enough in the morning.'

Ev wagged his reins and, as his mount started forward, Featherstone lost his practised calmness. When he spoke, his voice was several notches higher than it usually was.

'Carter, you son of a bitch. No one crosses me an' walks off smiling.'

Carter, like all horsemen, was holding his reins in his left hand. His right hand eased downward and stopped within inches of his holster when the medicine man spoke sharply to Featherstone. 'Be careful about calling people names; you can get someone killed.'

Featherstone turned on the doctor. 'What'd he agree to pay you?'

The physician was a man with a short fuse also. He wasn't armed, but physically he was a match for Featherstone and then some. He called Featherstone by his first name and followed that up in an angry denunciation.

'You get off that horse and I'll teach you some manners, you spindly little whelp. Go ahead! Get down!'

Featherstone made no move to dismount, but he fixed the medicine man with a look fit to squelch him. 'An' you witnessed it for Carter, did you?'

The physician eased up to dismount when the deputy sheriff fisted his sidearm and glared at the doctor without smiling. 'Set back. Now loosen up, all of you. Mr Featherstone let's go on down where you hired me to ride with you.'

Featherstone had the reins in his left hand in a knotted grip. The deputy leaned and struck Featherstone's horse a light slap with his own reins. The animal had been dozing. It jumped ahead nearly going out from under its rider. Featherstone set his horse up. It came to a sliding halt. The deputy leaned, but the horse could see his hand with the reins in it rising and jumped again. He looked back. 'Go on, Ev, *go on!*'

The doctor's horse moved out. Behind it, Ev's animal had seen those reins raised for the second slap. It didn't wait, it got in behind the doctor's animal and neither slackened its pace nor looked back.

When the separation was wider, Carter looked back and growled. 'That deputy saved that damned fool's life.'

The doctor said nothing. He was still fighting mad. They passed a dead or dying old cottonwood tree, known locally as the hang tree before the doctor found his normal voice. 'That scruffy son of a bitch. I've known him since I came here. He'd sell his soul and figure some way to cheat the Devil. Next time he needs me he can go to hell.'

By the time in late afternoon Carter and his companions got back where they'd ridden out, maybe a little shy of sunrise, all three of them were as hungry as bitch wolves.

While caring for their animals at the barn, Ev volunteered to rassle up a meal at the main house. Later, when they were eating, Agnes Courtright and her father rode in. The doctor stayed only long enough to exchange greetings then left.

Adam had never been inside the Morgan ranch's main house and was impressed. Despite fading daylight, Carter took Agnes on an escorted tour.

She, too, was impressed. Carter held her hand until they visited the horse barn where she freed her fingers when the big running horse poked his head out over the lower door for her to stroke his face. He closed his eyes in ecstasy and Carter laughed. He told Agnes he had never known a loving horse before. The broke horses he had known did what was required of them as long as they were fed and cared for in return.

He took her out back where his

buckskin was standing hip-shot outside the corral gate. He softly nickered and Carter opened the corral so he could go inside. He got a forkful of hay and pitched it over into the corral.

Agnes chuckled. 'And you think the running horse is a lovin' critter.'

Carter leaned on the fork looking at her. 'I didn't say other horses, like other people aren't also lovin' critters. By the way, I have a son.'

She stopped stone still. 'You're married?'

'Well, no. I *was* married. She died some years back.'

'Your son, how old would he be?'

'Goin' on fourteen, fifteen.'

'Where is he?'

'Down in Texas with my brother-in-law. I been thinkin' about maybe goin' after him an' bringin' him up here. Emily Morgan left me her ranch, wrote it out before she died. She wrote it out for the medicine man to give to me. Him, Ev an' I recorded the deed. Just got back this afternoon. The doctor went with us to take an oath that he witnessed her signin' the paper.'

Agnes hadn't moved since Carter had mentioned having a son. She continued to stand without moving when she said, 'Emily's dead an' you own her outfit?'

'Yes'm, lock, stock an' barrel.'

'An' how old did you say your son was?'

Carter saw no reason for that to interest her, but he answered anyway. 'Fourteen, fifteen, I'm not sure. When his mother died he was fairly young an' her brother and his wife took him in.'

Agnes relaxed a little. The chance of a boy who had grown up with people who'd been parents to him and be willing to take up with a father he'd never known would be unlikely.

Ev came along to say they had a hung-up calving cow out a ways. 'She's walkin' around, lies down, gets up an' walks. You comin'?'

Carter left Agnes and her father at the house. He told them he'd be back directly.

He rode his buckskin; the two of them had delivered many hung-up calves. Carter would have taken Brown Billy except that he did not know if Brown Billy had ever worked a rope.

It was not distant. Ev had seen the cow from the corral beyond the barn, but distance wasn't the issue. They loped out there. The cow saw them coming. She was a range animal, they just naturally tried to avoid horsemen.

It was losing race. Ev took down his rope, shook out a loop and hooked his horse into a run. When he was within a yard or such a matter, he made his cast. Any rangeman Ev's age doesn't miss. He set his horse up; when the slack went out of the rope, momentum made her swing around facing the riders. Ev kept his rope snug. The cow could breathe but she couldn't get clear.

Far behind a man yelled. Neither Carter nor Ev heeded the yell.

Carter came in behind the cow and Ev yanked her so that Carter could heel her, which he did, then both men backed their mounts until the old girl's tongue was out and she went down. Carter's heeling rope was snug to his saddle horn when he hit the ground.

The calf feebly kicked with its hind legs. Carter caught hold of both wet legs and waved with one hand. His buckskin horse sidled backwards slowly.

The calf hit the ground sucking air. Ev waited until Carter was back astride before flipping slack. The cow was fighting mad, she shed the rope and charged. Ev was ready and reined away in a lope. The cow slackened to a trot, watched Ev widen the distance between them and turned back where her newborn was fighting to stand on all fours. When she reached it and started to clean it with a sandpaper tongue, the calf went down and remained down. The cow ignored Ev and Carter. She also ignored the two Courtrights who flung dust when they halted nearby. Adam had his rope down. While watching the cow and calf he methodically coiled his rope.

Agnes rode over where Carter was blowing his horse and was doing as her father had done, coiling his wet lariat.

She said, 'Pa'll be satisfied.'

Carter looked blank when he replied, 'Will he?'

She reddened as she smiled. 'He's said many times he'd be almighty happy if a real stockman would get hold of the Morgan place. Carter?'

'Yes'm?'

'I'll fix something to eat,' she smiled, turned around and headed toward the house.

Carter remained fixed to the spot watching her until Ev walked up with his horse, eyed Carter, the girl walking away, then said, 'We'd better take care of the horses, Bob.'

After they had returned to the barn, off-saddled and forked hay, Ev said he would finish up the chores while Carter got cleaned up for supper.

13

A Near Miss

Carter was turning in the direction of the house when the moonless night was blown apart by two thunderous gun-shots.

Ev went down, rolled, got both hands under himself and pushed. He almost made it to his knees when he heard someone shouting and dropped flat out.

It was the big brown horse who helped. He had been taken from his stall and turned into the corral behind the barn. He ran in circles, stopped occasionally with his head over the topmost stringer. He wasn't making any noise, but each time he stopped he looked in the same direction. Ev knew about animals pointing and with a fisted sidearm went hurrying in that direction.

The sound of a man running after him almost caused a killing. Ev saw the dark shape of a sprawled man lying face down at the same moment he heard the oncoming man. He sank to one knee close to the sprawled individual and raised his pistol and cocked it. His finger was inside the trigger guard when the oncoming man called to him in a voice Ev recognized and eased up his pressure in the trigger guard.

'Adam! Over here!'

With practically no light, Adam Courtright came closer to the area of Ev's yell and stopped stone still as Ev stood up, leathered his six-gun and said, 'Help me get him to the house!'

Adam leaned down, pulled back and held up a bloody hand. He asked Ev if the face-down man was dead and Ev snarled his answer, 'Blood's still runnin'. Take hold! Talk later!'

Getting Carter to the house was nothing men would want to do for a living, and by the time they met Agnes in the doorway holding a lighted lamp aloft they had blood on their clothing and their hands.

They placed him flat out on the parlour floor and Adam yelled for Ev to go for the doctor; he and Agnes would try to do what they could to stop the bleeding.

Ev left the house heading for the barn. It wasn't long before he was on his way to town; not in his usual, regular lope, but in a dead run.

There were lights in Tumbleweed when Ev arrived there. The doctor was out setting a broken arm according to his wife, who assured Ev he would return soon. Ev wanted to know where the doctor was and his wife sidled around a direct reply by inviting Ev into the house to wait. With no choice, Ev entered the house, sat in the parlour waiting.

She was right. The doctor came in from out back where he'd forked feed to his horse. Ev told him in as few words as possible what had happened. The doctor nodded and said, 'I'll go out back an' rig out the horse. You wait for me out front, Ev.'

Ev waited out front beside his dozing mount. What seemed to take enough time to rig out five horses went by before the medicine man appeared.

They left Tumbleweed in a rocking lope and held to that gait for a considerable distance. By the time they could see lights at the Morgan place, the doctor asked if Ev cared for a drink and brought forth from his saddlebag a bottle of Johnny Walker. They drank on the move, turned in off the main road at a walk and held to it until they were in the barnyard where Ev offered to care for their animals.

The medicine man entered the parlour, knelt and called for more light, hot water and plenty of clean cloth.

Agnes stood like a statue with her lantern in one hand, the other hand to her mouth. She said, 'He's dead!'

The doctor was wiping his hands when he looked up and spoke irritably. 'He's not dead, but he will be. Hot water, Agnes, and all the clean towels you can find. Adam, cut the shirt off. Don't bother with the buttons, use your pocket knife. Carter, can you hear me?' When the prone man made no attempt to answer, the doctor told Agnes to help roll him on to one side.

She knelt to help but wasn't as much help as her father was in getting Carter where the doctor could finish his examination.

He rocked back on his heels, looked up for Ev and was the first to notice that the old rangeman had not come into the room.

The doctor worked with his lips sucked flat. When he needed help he growled. For a half-hour he was occupied with stopping the bleeding and probing until he found and extracted a bullet which, though not misshapen, had not quite emerged where it pushed against the flesh.

Extraction required more stoppage, more clean towels and time of which no one was aware even when the parlour got chilly.

Adam stood up. His back and legs would not stand for any more kneeling. He had the bullet in his hand. 'Doc,' he said quietly, 'there was two shots.'

The retort came from the hunched-over doctor in a sharp tone of voice. 'I can count, Adam, gawddammit!'

A little later, Adam spoke again. 'We could hoist him on to the couch.'

The answer came in the same irritable tone of voice. 'Sure we could — an' start the bleeding again.'

Adam left to stand on the porch. The night was silent, dark, and getting colder by the minute. He went to the barn for no particular reason, but Ev wasn't there.

Adam Courtright had been a soldier. The sight of torn flesh and blood made an impression, but since there was nothing he could do inside he thought of the bushwhacker. Without knowing which animal Ev normally rode he had to guess. There were two stalled horses and a door hanging open where a third horse had been stalled.

Adam returned to the house. The physician was drying his hands and arms. He put a quizzical look on Adam. 'Find anything?' he asked.

Adam sat down on a leather-bottomed chair shaking his head. 'Only that Ev ain't around.'

The doctor finished with his sleeves. 'You didn't expect to find him, did you? His kind takes bushwhackin' personal. I've known him quite a while. If he picks up tracks you can bet new money he's on a trail. Well, I've done all I can do. I got to get home. Adam, don't move this feller an' keep watch over him. My guess is that with decent care he'll make it. That second slug hit him in the butt. That bled like a stuck hawg. He won't be ridin' out for a long time.' Doc finished wiping, dropped the towel and said, 'Maybe your girl could mind him for a while.'

Adam accompanied the medicine man to the barn. They talked while Doc rigged out his animal and led it outside before mounting. His last words before he rode from the yard were a reiteration of something he'd mentioned before. 'If your girl could mind him for a few days . . .'

Adam had a question. 'You pretty sure he'll live, Doc?'

The doctor smiled. 'He's lost a sight of blood. He'll be weak as a kitten for a spell, but he'll make it . . . that is if the bushwhacker don't come back an' finish the job.'

Adam returned to the house and got a surprise. His daughter had made no attempt to move Carter but she had found a small rug to roll up to serve as a pillow and Carter seemed comfortable. They had been talking. Agnes had explained what she knew of the bushwhack and how Carter had been wounded. His gaze at Adam was clear, only when he moved did he show any expression. It was painful, but he did his best to hide that fact. He even forced a sweat-shiny grin when he asked Adam about Everett.

'Gone, Mr Carter. Took a horse an' went. Want me to guess?'

Carter barely inclined his head which Courtright interpreted correctly and said, 'Trackin' your bushwhacker.'

Carter's forced small smile lingered. 'In the dark?'

It was Adam's turn to show rugged humour. 'His kind can track a fly over a glass window.'

Agnes arose from beside Carter. She did this a trifle stiffly. She said she'd make some broth and went in the direction of the kitchen.

Carter had a question for her father. 'Ev say anything, like maybe he had an idea about the bushwhacker?'

'No. In fact, with all the other commotion I had no idea Ev had left. You better keep him on; accordin' to the medicine man you won't be fit to set a saddle for a spell. That slug that grazed your behind didn't go deep but it sure as hell ploughed a gash in both cheeks.'

'How about the other one?'

'It's a mean one, higher up and straight through you. It stopped just before comin' out through the skin. Doc removed it. I don't know about such things, but Doc thinks the bullet somehow or t'other missed all your workin' parts. How it'd do that I got no idea . . . maybe shootin' at night in the dark an' you mostly movin'.'

Agnes returned with two bowls of beef broth hotter than a June bride on a feather mattress, but the men breathed deeply of the aroma until they could empty the cups.

Adam went to build a fire. It was getting along toward the coldest part of the night.

When warmth circulated, Adam went to sleep in a chair and his daughter sat talking with Carter. If he had been sleepy the broth nixed it. Or maybe it was the pretty girl close to him on the parlour floor.

Dawn came slowly, first a pale-orange streak that gradually widened, then daylight and finally the brilliance of full daylight, and Carter slept.

Agnes made breakfast for herself and her father. Carter had a fever, no appetite and ached all over, worse than he had felt the night before.

Adam found an ivory-handled straight razor, a soap mug and a brush, all the items required for him to shave. He offered to shave Carter but he declined.

Aggie went to the barn area to pitch feed and do whatever other chores required daily attendance.

There was no sign of Everett. While she was outside, her father ignored Carter's garrulous complaints, got hot water and washed Carter's wounds and rebandaged them. When he finished he stood up with his hat on. He would come back, but he had to go home and do his own chores. He off-handedly said he'd leave his daughter in case Carter took a turn for the worse.

She exchanged a wave as her father rode out of the private ruts to the main thoroughfare and broke over into a lope for home.

To Carter's irritation, Agnes spent almost a full half-hour making herself presentable. She did not need that much time but she had her own reason for taking it.

This time when she sat on the floor beside Carter she brought a pillow. His bad mood did not last long when she came to sit with him.

They talked, joked, exchanged confidences and, with the sun directly overhead, she fed him. He ate because she smilingly insisted, not because he was the least bit hungry.

The afternoon was advancing when someone riding a horse turned in from the main road. Carter said it would be her father and as she started to arise and go to the door he said. 'Aggie, we've known each other quite a spell, wouldn't you say?'

She stood looking down at him from over by the door. 'I expect that'd be how a body figures time.'

He held her at the door with a very direct stare. 'I'd say long enough. We talked. I told you about me an' you told me about you growin' up an' all.'

'Bob, are you fixin' to say something?'

He started to move. The pain made him stop but his colour remained high. 'Well, me bein' laid up for a spell an' all . . . '

'An' you need someone to look after you?'

'That's not exactly what I was screwin' up my nerve to say, but that's a fact . . . Aggie?'

'Bob, I'm old enough. Whatever you're tryin' to say won't upset me.'

'Will you marry me?'

It didn't upset her, but for a fact it shocked her. She left the door closed came over to him, sank on both knees, leaned forward and did something no other female woman had done since he'd been younger. She kissed him squarely on the mouth.

They both blushed a fiery red. She

leaned back. 'When?'

He briefly pondered. 'Well, I can't stand up to face a preacher.'

'Something I expect no one ever told you . . . my mother's a preacher in our church over at the fort. Every Sunday that the road's open.'

Someone knocked on the door with a gloved fist, didn't wait, lifted the latch and walked in and stopped dead still, gaping as Agnes was bent far over from the waist and Carter raised up several inches for the kiss.

The visitor reached back and gave the door a rough push. It slammed with a reverberation that rattled the house.

Aggie jerked back as Carter recognized the visitor. He had thought it was Agnes's father. He said, 'Ev! Where in hell have you been?'

The old rangeman brought something from behind his back, came closer an' held out a freshly cleaned and oiled rifle which he held toward Carter.

'Hang it on the wall, Bob. It belonged to your bushwhacker. I wish you could've been there to hear the son of a bitch squeal.'

Agnes took the rifle. She was afraid Carter would move and start bleeding again if Ev handed it to him.

Carter and the older man looked steadily at each other as Ev said, 'I knew it had to be him, the connivin', scrawny bastard — excuse me, Aggie — the underhanded, double-dealin' weasel. You know what he was doin' when I walked in on him? He was cleanin' an' oilin' his bushwhacker's rifle so's there'd be no sign it'd been fired.'

Carter said, 'Him, Ev?'

'Sure as I'm standin' here. They'll be awhile findin' him. A gun'd be too noisy. I used my boot knife.'

Agnes stood in mild bewilderment until she said, 'Ev . . . who?'

Ev's retort was roughly given. 'Who? That thievin', forgin', lyin', land-stealin' Featherstone! With him dead an' out of the runnin', his forged deed to the Morgan place an' everythin' with it.

Bob, I'd put his bushwhackin' gun out of sight. Cassidy's fat an' likes his livin' not to be upset by things like this. A spell of gossip an' they'll bury that . . . feller, and forget he fell on a knife.'

When Adam returned, with dusk fading toward night, Agnes explained what Ev had done, had been able to figure who the bushwhacker was by instinct. Adam nodded his agreement.

Agnes was enormously relieved, even more so when he said her mother had fed him before he left to return. She wouldn't have to feed her father and just the mention of food made Carter lose colour.

By the following morning, when Sheriff Cassidy arrived in his top buggy, he was dumbfounded. He'd had no idea there had been a shooting the day before. He did know about Featherstone falling on a knife, but that was less significant than Carter's injury. He pressed hard for an explanation and got the same answer from Carter and his house guests. It was getting dark when the shooting had occurred. Too dark to see and identify the bushwhacker. He agreed with Ev and Adam the killing of Featherstone was certainly quite a coincidence, him dying soon after Carter and Ev returned from recording the deed at the county seat, but, as the sheriff opined, coincidences did happen, not often, but they occurred and Cassidy acted less troubled than satisfied. As he said, 'Bob Carter's only hint of a cloud on his deed of ownership has died with its other claimant.' Cassidy said he'd ridden out to congratulate Carter on ownership. He had no idea the people in the parlour with Carter knew about Featherstone's passing hours before he heard about it.

There was another visitor from town: Tom Leary, the general store owner from town. It appeared that Emily Morgan had run up a bill at Leary's store for several months. Sixty-six dollars' worth. He never made it to the house. Ev intercepted him when Leary led his saddle animal to the barn to be stalled while he conducted business. Leary was a high-strung man who carried no more than half-a-dozen customers and with Emily Morgan's passing he had worked himself into a fit because, as he told Ev at the barn, when folks died owing the store, it wasn't always possible to collect owed debts.

Ev raised a hand to prevent Leary from going to the main house. As he did this he fished under his trouser belt, his shell belt, and worried loose a money belt.

Under the astonished stare of the storekeeper, he opened one pocket on the belt, removed a fat pad of greenbacks, very methodically counted out sixty-six wrinkled greenbacks, handed them to the storekeeper whose eyes were wide, and told Leary that Carter had been injured and was in the house with Adam Courtright and his daughter, and it wouldn't set well if Leary burst in to present his claim.

Leary counted the money, pocketed

it as he said, 'Ev, that's a lot of money. You reckon you'll get it back?'

The old rangeman grinned. 'Don't you worry none, Tom.'

'Well, tell Mr Carter I hope he gets well an' fit right soon.'

Ev led the storekeeper's animal out to be mounted. The only diversion was that Ev led the animal to drink at the trough first.

As Leary scrambled into the saddle, he gave Ev another puzzled look, raised his hand in a salute and left the yard at a steady walk. Ev lingered at the barn until the storekeeper was well on his way back to town then went over to the house where Agnes asked if she hadn't seen the storekeeper ride in.

Ev's retort was calmly given. 'Yes'm. He come to give his condolences. I told him you folks was with Carter an' he was too sick to have visitors.'

Other titles in the
Linford Western Library:

DEAD IS FOR EVER

Amy Sadler

After rescuing Hope Bennett from the clutches of two trailbums, Sam Carver made a serious mistake. He killed one of the outlaws, and reckoned on collecting the bounty on Lew Daggett. But catching Sam off-guard, Daggett made off with the girl, leaving Sam for dead. However, he was only grazed and once he came to, he set out in search of Hope. When he eventually found her, he was forced into a dramatic showdown with his life on the line.

SMOKING STAR

B. J. Holmes

In the one-horse town of Medicine Bluff two men were dead. Sheriff Jack Starr didn't need the badge on his chest to spur him into tracking the killer. He had his own reason for seeking justice, a reason no-one knew. It drove him to take a journey into the past where he was to discover something else that was to add even greater urgency to the situation — to stop Montana's rivers running red with blood.

CABEL

Paul K. McAfee

Josh Cabel returned home from the Civil War to find his family all murdered by rioting members of Quantrill's band. The hunt for the killers led Josh to Colorado City where, after months of searching, he finally settled down to work on a ranch nearby. He saved the life of an Indian, who led him to a cache of weapons waiting for Sitting Bull's attack on the Whites. His involvement threw Cabel into grave danger. When the final confrontation came, who had the fastest — and deadlier — draw?

RIVERBOAT

Alan C. Porter

When Rufus Blake died he was found to be carrying a gold bar from a Confederate gold shipment that had disappeared twenty years before. This inspires Wes Hardiman and Ben Travis to swap horse and trail for a riverboat, the *River Queen*, on the Mississippi, in an effort to find the missing gold. Cord Duval is set on destroying the *River Queen* and he has the power and the gunmen to do it. Guns blaze as Hardiman and Travis attempt to unravel the mystery and stay alive.